THE LONG DEAD

DEAD

A British murder mystery with detective John
Blizzard

JOHN DEAN

THE
BOOK
FOLKS

Paperback published by The Book Folks

London, 2017

© John Dean

ISBN 978-1-5499-0364-9

www.thebookfolks.com

The Long Dead is the first in a series of British detective novels featuring Detective Chief Inspector John Blizzard. Look out for the other books in the series: Strange Little Girl, The Railway Man and The Secrets Man.

Chapter one

'There's something very badly wrong here,' said John Blizzard.

Brow furrowed, he looked up from his intense study of the ground and stared through the murk of the late afternoon mist at the bare winter fields stretching away into the distance. The grey shroud that had enveloped the countryside around the city of Hafton for days was thickening rapidly once more as dusk approached and the fog was rolling noiselessly in over copse and hedgerow. As he watched the fields disappear, the detective chief inspector was suddenly struck by how alone he and Detective Sergeant David Colley were as they stood on the edge of the makeshift grave.

Something caught him off-guard. As Blizzard stared into the swirling fog, he felt for a moment, just a fleeting moment, an overwhelming sense of a past long gone. He could feel, almost as if it were physical, the acute pain of loss, the pain of those left to grieve for loved ones long departed. And he saw through the mist the indistinct image of a man's face; the dark hair cropped short, the smile crooked and knowing, the expression open and care-free, the eyes glinting with the merest hint of mischief, an image locked in memory and frozen in time on a tattered black-and-white photograph.

For a moment, the man's expression changed and Blizzard was transported to a wild place, the man's place, and heard the roar and the clatter, felt the panic as the man fought for his life, heard the death rattle of his final breath. Saw in his face the pain, a different pain, the pain that comes with fear and defeat. The defeat of a man who knew he could never go home, would never see his loved ones again, would never feel the warmth of the evening summer sun on his back or feel the trusting embrace of a child. A man alone and unheard, yet not un-mourned. No, not un-mourned. And not forgotten. At the going down of the sun and in the morning, we will remember them. Remember them all. And in that moment, John Blizzard remembered the man. And mourned him.

Then the face was gone, receding into the mist, and with a start, John Blizzard was back in the icy chill of a November afternoon, standing on the fringes of a field and staring into a grave. Startled at what he had seen, or thought he had seen, the chief inspector shook his head to banish the images from his mind, and noticed Colley looking at him oddly.

'This damned fog,' said Blizzard gruffly.

A questioning look from the sergeant.

'Plays tricks,' said the chief inspector, embarrassed at having let his guard down.

'Tricks?'

'Nothing. It's just…' Blizzard shrugged. 'I don't know, it's difficult to put into words…'

'Try,' said Colley.

'Like I said, it's just something's wrong. Something here. I feel it so strongly, David,' said Blizzard, surprising himself with the vehemence of his words.

'Not sure I understand, guv.'

'Neither do I but this place is speaking to me. It's quite, I don't know…' Blizzard shrugged. 'Unnerving.'

'Unnerved? You?' Colley looked at his colleague in amazement.

Over the years, he and Blizzard had stood and stared down at many a body – too many for their liking – and the sergeant had never heard the chief inspector talk like this, never seen such a strange expression on his face, never. As Blizzard had said many times, with a wry smile, the living might sometimes scare him but the dead sure as hell did not. They could not harm anyone now, so why worry about them? It was one of his favourite sayings and Colley had lost count of the number of times he had heard it. But that was then and this was now – and now the dead had affected Blizzard and made him uneasy. And if John Blizzard was uneasy, that meant David Colley was uneasy as well.

What was more confusing for the sergeant was that when, shortly after three that afternoon, they arrived at Green Meadow Farm, deep into the rural flatlands five miles to the west of the city, he had not felt that way at all. There had been no bunching in the gut, no unpleasant taste at the back of the throat like he had experienced so many times on the way to a death. No, this one was as straightforward as they come. All those bodies and none of them his problem, the sergeant had thought cheerfully as he struggled out of the car and into his blue windcheater before following Blizzard, who was already striding up the farm track. No arduous paperwork, no grieving relatives, no agitated top brass demanding updates on the inquiry, nothing to worry about, the sergeant had told himself as he fell into step with the chief inspector, their feet crunching on the frozen ruts. Indeed, thought the sergeant as they turned through a gate and walked without speaking across the meadow, it was looking good for an early Friday night finish and a pleasant night out with his girlfriend, Jay.

The sergeant was wondering if he had somehow missed something. He looked down again and pondered the skeletons laid out before them. They were in a long line, placed neatly side by side in a large hole in the ground; to call it a grave would be granting it too much dignity. Running parallel with the raggedy hedge and without a headstone to identify the location half way along the field, the hole had been discovered by workmen doing drainage excavation. The bodies, which had been placed on their backs, looked like they were many years old, the flesh long since rotted off bones to which clung obstinate tatters of grubby material. Around their necks were metal tags bearing their names. German names.

Colley looked thoughtfully at the laughing skulls staring up into the gloom of a fading winter's day. There were sixteen bodies in all. Colley knew that, he had counted them three times. One didn't normally need to do that with deaths but this case was different. He had not examined them particularly closely. They were long dead, he thought, and no concern of the police. Part of history. Part of military history, indeed. The name tags had confirmed their identities; these were men who rested in cold silence a long way from home, having given their lives for their country. Proud men who, more than fifty years before, had left wives and children, mothers and fathers, and headed to war with such optimism, only to perish on the edge of a bleak northern English city, the rousing patriotic songs of their departures long since choked in throats clogged by the soil of England.

Sad, sure, but for Colley, who had never been fascinated by war, it meant little. To him, it was history and nothing more. Maybe, he mused, reflecting on the chief inspector's reaction a few seconds before, it was Blizzard's keen interest in history that imbued the scene with extra significance for him. Thinking of Blizzard brought forth a little involuntary shake of the head from the sergeant. No, he could not see it, this was not evil, this was a routine job and the detectives were simply there to make sure all the rules were followed and that the paperwork could be filled in. A quirky case for the N.F.A file. Something to tell the lads over a pint, then move on. Nothing more. No, definitely nothing more.

The sergeant looked up and morosely surveyed the skeletal hedgerow, the damp and wispy grassy field margins, the black claw-fingered trees and the bare earth with its barren ridges and furrows stretching away into the mist. He shivered, suddenly acutely conscious of how cold he had become in the damp late afternoon chill. Oh, what he would give for a warming cuppa, and he glanced enviously across the fields to the distant farmhouse with its welcoming lights glowing ever brighter in the deepening gloom.

'Are we done?' asked the sergeant hopefully, looking at the chief inspector, who was still staring into the grave.

'No, David, I do not think we are.'

'But it's straightforward, guv.'

'Don't think so. Something wicked happened here.'

'Not according to the archaeologists, guv.'

Colley knew the archaeologists were sitting in the farmer's kitchen and he could almost feel, behind the steamed-up windows, the heat rising from their mugs of tea and hear their laughter and chatter. He glanced at the distant farmhouse wistfully again while Blizzard pondered the comment. It was the archaeologists who called in the police the moment the bodies had been unearthed. The team, seconded from a Midlands university by English Heritage, had been working several hundred yards away from the graves for almost four months, painstakingly exploring the faded green wooden huts arranged in three neat rows that were once Hafton Prisoner-Of-War Camp.

Home at any one time during the 1940s to as many as 600 captured German soldiers, the 24 huts had fallen into disrepair following the camp's closure when peace returned to Europe. They stood largely unnoticed for the following decades, used to house tractors and store animal feed, and increasingly obscured from sight by the alder trees and scrubby bushes that had grown around them. Their existence was brought to public attention again when it was revealed that the landowner, a farmer called

Henderson Ramage, was seeking to sell part of his land for a housing development.

The revelation provoked fury among local people and a protest committee was quickly assembled, villagers voicing their anger at noisy public meetings in nearby Hawkwith village and outside city hall whenever planning councillors debated the issue. Within a month of Ramage's plans becoming public, a housebuilder expressed an interest in the site, planning applications were submitted, rejected and re-submitted and in the end, after a final refusal by the council, the decision was referred by the city council to a planning inquiry. After a two-week hearing, the government inspector finally recommended approval but the housebuilder went into liquidation before work began and nothing had happened on the site for years. Now the plan had been revived, larger than before and with a new housebuilder.

It was a young council officer on a routine visit to the site who suggested that there was an opportunity to investigate the huts before the work started. Realising the importance of the eight-acre site, the officer informed English Heritage, whose experts announced they were keen to see the camp preserved and were alarmed that the edge of the proposed new extended housing development came perilously close to the huts. Loathe to submit themselves to further delays, Henderson Ramage and the housebuilder initially refused to co-operate with an investigation but faced with a mixture of cajoling and legal threats, they reluctantly relented.

The six-strong university team, including four students, restricted themselves to the camp itself, so it was a digger driver excavating a drainage ditch who stumbled across its secret. To his horror, he unearthed the bodies when he plunged his scoop into the crusty soil to reveal a bony hand clawing the air for the first time in half a century.

'So, what do we do now?' asked the sergeant.

'I think…' Blizzard paused on hearing a footfall.

They turned to see a man walking across the field, his identity obscured by his anorak hood. As he approached, they could see he was the lead archaeologist, Dr Richard Hamer, a tall, thin and sallow man with a nose that was long and hooked, sunken cheeks, eyes which were dark and strangely lifeless, and teeth that were prominent and jutting out.

'Marvellous,' said Colley, 'here comes Dracula.'

'Respect. That's Mr Dracula to the likes of you.'

'Probably only comes out at night,' said Colley, glancing up at the darkening sky as the archaeologist neared.

'So, can we have them back?' asked Hamer, nodding at the grave.

'I am afraid not,' said Blizzard.

'Why?'

'I want our forensic team to have a look.'

'Why on earth would you want to do that?'

'I'm not satisfied,' said Blizzard.

'Oh, come on. This is routine, we all know that.'

'You may jump to conclusions in your profession but we do not,' said Blizzard.

'Uncalled for,' replied Hamer. 'We pride ourselves on our thoroughness, but let us be sensible about this, Chief Inspector. This is an old burial site. There can be no doubt about it. Our research has confirmed that in the winter of 1944-45, there was in influenza epidemic that killed a number of the POWs.'

'Then why were they buried here?' asked Blizzard. 'And not in a local churchyard?'

'Maybe the churches did not want to take them for fear of spreading the virus.'

'And why so far outside the camp?'

'Probably the same reason,' said Hamer. 'Anyway, it is not really important.'

'I think it is,' said Blizzard.

'Surely the local constabulary has got better things to do than investigate deaths from natural causes. I mean, isn't there some poor motorist you should be out hassling?'

Colley watched the chief inspector with anticipation; Blizzard had reduced men to tears for less. This time, however, the reaction was not explosive. The chief inspector considered the comment for a moment then smiled at the archaeologist. Colley knew the smile well. For some reason, it always reminded him of a lion just before it ate its prey.

'You know, Mr Hamer…' began Blizzard.

'Doctor Hamer, it's *Doctor* Hamer.'

'Well whatever you call yourself,' said Blizzard, starting to walk away across the field. 'Until I am happy about this, these bodies are mine.'

Gloomily, Hamer watched him go, then glanced at the sergeant with a questioning look on his face.

'When the man ain't happy,' said Colley, 'the man ain't happy.'

'Is he ever?'

'Oh, yes, back in 2005 I think it was. Christmas-time. Oh, no, hang on, that can't be right, the guvn'r hates Christmas.'

Chuckling, Colley walked off to organise an all-night guard for the grave, leaving the bemused Doctor Hamer standing alone in the field with only his thoughts and the ghosts of sixteen dead men for company.

Chapter two

'OK,' said John Blizzard. He leaned forward and rested his elbows on the desk. 'Tell me there is nothing wrong with that burial site, tell me I haven't lost control of my senses.'

It was the following Monday morning and none of the five people in his office at Abbey Road Police Station were about to start the week by doing something that ill-advised. Even the archaeologists kept their doubts to themselves. Dr Hamer, perhaps sensing safety in numbers, had brought his colleague, the nervous-looking 28-year-old military archaeologist Elspeth Roberts, to the meeting.

Colley took a couple of moments to peruse the two other people completing the gathering crammed into the small office. As he looked at Peter Reynolds, the ghost of a smile played on the sergeant's lips, the presence of the Home Office pathologist always guaranteed good sport. Reynolds knew that Blizzard had never liked him. Next to him, his excitement hardly suppressed, was Detective Inspector Graham Ross, divisional head of forensics at Abbey Road Police Station, dressed as immaculately as ever.

'Well?' asked Blizzard, irritated by the smug expressions on the faces of Reynolds and Ross. 'Have I taken leave of my senses?'

'I hate to say it,' said Peter Reynolds, 'but you have not, and I speak as someone who would happily have signed the papers to have you sectioned many years ago.'

'Thank you for the sentiment,' murmured Blizzard. 'So, what have you found?'

'There is indeed something very wrong with the grave,' said Reynolds.

'He's right, guv,' said Graham Ross, unable to contain himself any longer. 'We're looking at a murder!'

'That is a preposterous statement!' exclaimed Hamer. 'And even if…'

'There will be plenty of time for your comments later,' said the chief inspector. 'Perhaps. But for the moment, who's murder are we looking at?'

'I am coming to that,' said the pathologist. 'Having spent my weekend examining the skeletons, and missing out on a good game of golf, might I say…'

'No, you may not,' grunted Blizzard.

'You are such a delightful man,' said Reynolds. 'Anyway, Mr Hamer here…'

'Actually, it's *Doctor* Hamer,' said the archaeologist.

'Yes, well whatever he is,' said Reynolds, fishing out some papers from his battered briefcase. 'He gave me names of the POWs from the camp.'

'And?' asked the chief inspector.

'I have to say first that proving the identity beyond all doubt will be extremely difficult after all these years,' said the pathologist. 'But the name tags on the skeletons do match the recorded names of POWs who died of influenza in the winter of 1944/45. Examination of the skeletons confirms that they date from around that time. It's the same with all fifteen of them.'

'Fifteen?' queried Blizzard. 'I thought there were sixteen?'

'Indeed there are,' said Reynolds. 'Although it is difficult to be absolutely precise, I would say number sixteen died ten to fifteen years ago.'

Reynolds sat back in his chair and, with a smug look on his face, waited for the reaction. It came within the blink of an eye.

'Bloody hell's bells!' exclaimed Blizzard.

'Indeed,' said Reynolds.

'So are you saying he was never a POW at the camp?' asked Colley, equally taken aback.

'That's the weird thing,' said Reynolds, holding up a brown file. 'According to the camp records, Horst Knoefler *was* an inmate and was released sometime in early 1946, not long before the camp closed. And he seems to have been alive and well when he walked out of the front gate.'

'And he was the murdered one, was he?' asked Blizzard.

'Indeed he was,' said Reynolds. 'There can be no doubt that, not only did our Herr Knoefler somehow clamber into that grave all those years after his comrades in arms, but it seems that someone gave him a helping hand.'

The atmosphere in the office was electric and Reynolds and Ross revelled in the astonished look on Blizzard's face as he tried to digest their revelations. It took a lot to surprise the chief inspector so such moments were to be enjoyed with relish; it might be a long time before one came again. Blizzard glanced at his sergeant.

'So I was right, David,' he said. 'Something was wrong.'

'So it would seem, guv,' said Colley, turning to Hamer. 'Can I ask where the records of the POWs came from? I mean, are we sure they are genuine?'

'We believe so,' said Hamer, trying to recover his own composure. 'Two of our researchers found them among papers in the local history section of the city library. They had been there for many years, gathering dust without anyone taking much notice of them.'

'That's archaeologists for you,' said Blizzard.

'I meant the papers had been there for years,' replied Hamer tartly.

'Of course, you did,' said Blizzard.

'So, how was he murdered, Mr Reynolds?' asked Colley.

'See that?' said Reynolds, shooting a sly look at Blizzard. 'Such politeness. Most refreshing in the young. Maybe it's a generation thing, Chief Inspector.'

'Just tell us the sodding cause of death,' grunted Blizzard.

'A blow to the back of the head. The skull shows signs of significant trauma and there is an unmistakeable sign of a fracture.'

'Any idea what he was struck with?'

'Could be anything, a block of wood, a shovel, a sledgehammer, a piece of rock. Whatever it was, it was wielded with enough force to kill him pretty much instantly, I would say.'

'Graham,' said Blizzard, glancing at the forensics chief, 'I take it our Mr Reynolds has not embarked on a flight of fancy?'

'Not sure he does flights of fancy but there's not much doubt about it.'

'Yeah, but how do we know?' insisted Colley. 'I mean, couldn't this Knoefler fellow have been murdered in 1945 and dumped in there with the others at the time?'

'Exactly,' said Hamer fervently, recognising a way of getting his people back onto the site.

'We thought of that,' said Ross. 'We examined the rotted material on the bones. It took a while as it was in a real mess but we are sure the fifteen were wearing camp uniforms whereas Knoefler was wearing modern clothes, possibly a dark pullover of some kind and slacks. And his shoes were modern. Very nice actually, very stylish, wouldn't have minded wearing them myself.'

'Thank you, Versace,' grunted Blizzard. 'But how do we know who he is? Surely he was not still wearing his name tag after all these years?'

'No, he wasn't, but he was wearing a watch that had his name engraved on the back.'

'A name, yes,' said Blizzard. 'But that does not necessarily mean that it is *his* name. Is it possible that he is not Horst Knoefler?'

'Yes, of course it is, but for the moment it's all we have to go on so I, for one, am going to call him Horst Knoefler.'

There were a few moments of silence as everyone digested what they had heard.

'So what do you reckon?' asked Colley at length, looking at the thoughtful chief inspector.

'It is certainly intriguing,' mused Blizzard, leaning back in his chair with a look of satisfaction on his face.

'I assume that means we cannot examine the graves any further?' asked Hamer gloomily.

'Or the camp. It is now all a potential murder scene,' said Blizzard. 'And it's all mine until I tell you different. DI Ross here will want to spend more time out there and the last thing he wants is you running about with your clipboards.'

'I must protest,' exclaimed Hamer, half standing up. 'There is important historical research that we need to do there before the…'

'Protest all you like,' snapped Blizzard. 'But when it comes to murder, my needs take precedence over a bunch of archaeologists.'

He looked at Elspeth Roberts, who had sat through the meeting with ever-widening eyes.

'You have been very quiet, Mrs Roberts,' said the chief inspector. 'Your colleague here insisted you be present at this meeting because of your expert knowledge.

Do you have anything to say which might throw some light onto this somewhat strange occurrence?'

She looked at him, an anxious look on her face. For a moment, it seemed that the words had choked in her throat but somehow she managed to regain what little composure remained, and opened her mouth.

'Well,' she said, her voice tremulous with nerves, her hand anxiously twisting and untwisting her wedding ring, 'it does rather make you wonder.'

'Wonder what?' asked Blizzard, fixing her with one of his stern looks.

'Well.' She was now well and truly flustered. 'Wonder what happened, I suppose.'

She looked around the room unhappily. 'I mean,' she said. 'Doesn't it?' Her voice tailed off and she flushed red as she noticed everyone in the room staring at her, apart from an embarrassed Hamer, who looked downwards, seemingly suddenly fascinated with his shoes. Colley glanced at the chief inspector.

'Such wise words in one so young,' said Blizzard, with a faint twitch of the lips as he stood up and walked over to the window.

'Still,' he said brightly, turning back into the room, 'it's always good to have an expert in on these little shindigs, isn't it boys?'

Colley tried to stifle his laugh but failed.

Chapter three

'This gets stranger and stranger,' said Colley, walking into Detective Chief Superintendent Arthur Ronald's office without knocking, and tossing a brown file onto the desk.

'You sound like something out of Alice in Wonderland,' said Blizzard, who was sitting at the desk with his boss. 'I expect the sodding white rabbit to come running past any minute.'

'You'd only arrest him,' said Colley.

It was three thirty that afternoon and the chief inspector and Ronald, his direct superior at Abbey Road, were taking a break from the intense pressures brought about by the opening of a murder inquiry.

'How could it possibly get stranger?' asked Ronald, looking up at the sergeant as he slumped in a chair in the corner of the room.

'It's all down to man's best friend.'

Noticing their bemused expressions, Colley grinned.

'Wuff-wuff,' he said, putting his hands together in front of his face and making panting sounds.

'Have you the faintest idea what he is talking about?' asked Ronald, glancing at Blizzard.

'Not usually,' said the chief inspector.

His face broke into a rare smile as he saw the superintendent's expression. Blizzard and Ronald went back more than 20 years, having first worked together as rookie uniform officers before their careers took different paths. The men had been reunited at Abbey Road when Ronald assumed command of CID in the area and demanded Blizzard be moved from the drugs squad and promoted as his new detective chief inspector in Western Division. Not everyone in the corridors of power welcomed the idea. Indeed, some resisted it fiercely because Blizzard's brusque style had never endeared him to many at headquarters. Ronald viewed it as one of those things which had to be borne if you wanted the best. And Western CID had cut crime by more than a fifth in the mixture of its urban and rural areas.

They were very different men. University-educated Ronald, married with two teenaged children, was a slightly pudgy, balding man with ruddy cheeks and eyes with bags which sagged darkly. Given to constant worrying about mortgages and university fees, and a little prone, in Blizzard's view, to taking too much notice about what other people thought about him, he was not yet fifty but looked older.

'Perhaps you would like to explain the dog impression,' said Blizzard, picking up the file from the desk and glancing at the front cover. 'I seem to recall the name Willy Ramage – I assume he is related to Henderson?'

'Yeah, his father. He was shot dead by his dog.'

'He was indeed,' said Ronald. 'Fifteen years ago, if I remember correctly. It was bizarre. Everyone thought he had been murdered…'

'Yeah, I remember the case now,' said Blizzard. 'But it was not one of ours, surely? I thought it happened over towards Burniston. You were there, weren't you, Arthur?'

'I was indeed. The case was handled by our CID. DI Wheatley, if I am not mistaken.'

'It was,' said Colley. 'In fact, I have just come off the phone with him.'

'How is Danny?' asked Ronald. 'He's still in traffic, isn't he?'

'Yeah.'

'Such a waste,' said Blizzard, earning himself a disapproving look from the superintendent, who had at one point been in charge of the area's traffic section.

'You had better watch what you say about him,' warned Ronald. 'They reckon Danny Wheatley will be a chief superintendent within five years. He's the Chief Constable's blue-eyed boy, remember.'

'And there was me thinking I was,' said Blizzard innocently. 'It would explain why I didn't get a Christmas card from him last year. Mind, I'm not surprised Danny's done well, he was always very good at shuffling paper clips as I recall.'

Ronald let the comment go.

'Anyway,' said Colley, 'it was Danny who told me all about Willy Ramage and the link with Green Meadow Farm.'

It had been a sensational story at the time. Willy Ramage was a typical north country farmer. A man of few words and even fewer airs and graces, he had grown arable crops and kept a dairy herd at Green Meadow for nearly forty years, like his father and grandfather before him. Over time, Ramage had developed his business until he was able to purchase a second farm at Burniston, ten miles to the north of Green Meadow. He moved his family there because the farmhouse was much bigger; his son Henderson, daughter-in-law and their two children lived with the Ramages and the house had become too cramped. Willy Ramage left Green Meadow to be run by a tenant farmer.

One crisp winter morning, Willy went out on his customary early morning walk around his lands at Burniston, with his constant companion Ben, a black retriever, trotting by his side. They were after crows and Ramage had his shotgun with him as usual. By lunchtime, he still had not returned and Henderson and one of the farmhands went looking for him. They found Willy Ramage sprawled in a copse, trusty dog by his side, guarding the body. The police quickly confirmed that Ramage had sustained a massive shotgun injury to the leg and bled to death. There were signs that, although gravely injured, he had tried desperately to drag himself along the ground in the direction of the farmhouse a mile away. Initially, DI Danny Wheatley and his team treated it as a murder-style inquiry but forensic studies of the angle of the shotgun blast and markings on the ground led them to conclude that Willy had shot himself, the cartridge perhaps ricocheting off the hardened icy ground and tearing into his leg. Given that there was nothing in his life to suggest that he would want to kill himself, they came to the conclusion that he stumbled while walking through the copse and that the gun went off. Finding nothing else to explain such a stumble, they formulated the theory that in some way the dog impeded him, perhaps running across his path or jumping up. The story made headlines the world over.

'And it all happened about the same time our Mr Knoefler was dumped in the grave on Ramage's land,' said Colley.

'Like you say,' said Blizzard, 'it gets stranger and stranger. And you know, I am sure I recognise the name Henderson Ramage from somewhere else as well.'

'Got form for handling stolen goods and a couple of nasty assaults. He glassed a bloke in one of them. Bloke ended up being given seven pints of blood.'

'He's a nasty bit of work is Henderson Ramage,' said Ronald. 'When I was at Burniston, Danny Wheatley had him in on several occasions.'

'Yeah,' said Colley. 'Most of it happened in Burniston's patch. Danny gave me the low-down. Besides,

I've had dealings with Henderson Ramage myself over here.'

'I'm sure one of our lot investigated Henderson Ramage when I was on the drugs squad as well,' added Blizzard.

'Probably did,' said Colley. 'He's got form for a bit of heroin dealing. Nothing big-time though.'

'Did any of the offences take place at Green Meadow Farm?' asked Ronald.

'No,' said Colley. 'But one happened at the Burniston farm eight years ago. CID found him storing stolen tractor parts and a couple of half-inched quad bikes in one of the sheds. Ramage claimed he did not know how they got there.'

'It's those blessed fairies again,' murmured Blizzard.

'Must have been. They've got a lot to answer for. Anyway, he coughed to it.'

'And what did he get for that?' asked the chief inspector.

'Three months. Got out in five weeks apparently. Good behaviour.'

'Marvellous,' snorted Blizzard.

'Actually, it was not that bad,' said Colley. 'One of the quad bikes was lifted from a neighbouring farm – the words "shit" and "nest" spring readily to mind. When he got out, the farm lads went round to hold a lively discussion on the rights and wrongs of property ownership with our Henderson. Gave him such a beating, his skull thought it was a bagatelle machine. 'Ker-ching, ker-ching!'

'I take it he means a criminal assault upon Mr Ramage's person took place?' asked Roland.

'I believe so,' said Blizzard. 'Although Colley-speak can be a difficult language to translate into English. I'm thinking of running a course on it for beginners. You might want to enrol, Arthur.'

The sergeant grinned at Ronald's perplexed expression; he loved winding the superintendent up and the senior officer, for his part, knew it was the price he paid for having a damned good detective on the team.

'I take it Henderson still owns Green Meadow Farm?' asked Blizzard.

'Yeah, most of it,' said Colley. 'Apart, of course, from the bit he offered to the housebuilders. And that caused a bit of a fuss as well. I've sent Freddy Furnell to do some door-to-door in Hawkwith to see if he can turn anything juicy up from the locals.'

'Good stuff,' said Blizzard. 'How are we doing with our Herr Knoefler?'

'Not so well. I put a call into the German Embassy in London this morning but they have not been able to turn anything up yet. They seemed to think they would, given a little time. She was a very nice girl, I talked to, mind, guv. Sounded busty.'

'I'm sure she did,' said Blizzard with a smile.

'Anyhow,' said Colley. 'Forgot Knoefler for the moment, I'm not finished about Green Meadow Farm. See, I got to thinking about Henderson Ramage.'

'I can see why,' said Ronald. 'He's got to be worth a pull, hasn't he, John?'

Blizzard nodded.

'Then what are we waiting for?' asked Ronald. 'Let's bring him in.'

'In which case, sir,' said Colley, 'you might like to know that among Henderson's little mates is none other than one of the chief inspector's oldest and much-valued friends. In fact, it'll be a truly touching reunion.'

Blizzard raised a questioning eyebrow.

'Go on,' said Ronald cautiously, suspecting a sting in the tail to the comment.

It was duly delivered.

'Eddie Gayle,' said Colley.

'Marvellous,' said Ronald, raising his eyes to the ceiling. 'That's all we need.'

Blizzard beamed.

Chapter four

Fat, short and perspiring, Eddie Gayle somehow reminded Colley of a little round pig as he sat in the cramped interview room at Abbey Road Police Station late that afternoon. What was it with him and animal metaphors lately, thought the sergeant idly as he waited for the interview to begin. Then he remembered; a few days before, Jay had been telling him over dinner about a project that her young class were doing. Twenty-eight nine-year-olds producing drawings and writing stories on the theme of animals. And Jay said he never listened! The sergeant chuckled. Sitting next to him at the desk, and glancing quizzically at him when he heard the low laugh, was John Blizzard, the chief inspector's eyes bright – clearly relishing the opportunity to confront an old adversary.

Gayle, aged in his mid-forties, thinning black hair covered by a poorly-fitting wig and dressed as ever in a sharp dark suit which would have looked good on anyone else, glared back at the officers. He mopped his brow in the oppressive heat of the small room, the police station central heating system having continued to malfunction throughout the day. Cold as an ice box when the day shift reported for duty, the prefabs were now broiling. Colley, himself feeling uncomfortable in the heat beneath his sharply dressed exterior, noticed the flecks of dandruff on Gayle's jacket, the sweat rings round its armpits and the ugly red food stain on the pale blue tie. All in, Eddie Gayle did not present an appetising sight, and the sight of him perspiring gave the sergeant grim satisfaction. Blizzard's first rule of interviewing, he thought: make them sweat. Indeed, on more than one occasion, the chief inspector had been known to turn the radiator up in the interview room.

Gayle was well known to the police. He was a low-life, a man who stalked the gutters of the city, spreading his own brand of fear and hatred. And yet he had proved, so far at least, an 'untouchable' for the police, even though Blizzard and his detectives had been after him for years. Gayle's ability to twist and turn out of the very tightest of spots had long been a source of growing infuriation for Blizzard and Colley. Gayle's 'legitimate' business, the outwardly respectable façade behind which he sheltered, was property. Preferring to present himself to the public as a man of great standing within the community, he was the owner of many of the city's beautiful Victorian houses and liked to claim that he was helping to ease Hafton's acute accommodation crisis.

But successful entrepreneur was only the face that Eddie Gayle presented to the world. His real business was much darker; it was about making money whatever the cost to other people. Behind what little respectability his flash motors and cheap suits afforded him, Gayle was a selfish and nasty man, as well as being a crook and a thug.

For all the persistent rumours, pinning him down had proved virtually impossible and every time he walked free Eddie Gayle's confidence grew, the mocking smile became wider and his bravado more pronounced.

In the interview room that afternoon to ensure the chief inspector showed due respect was Paul D'Arcy, himself no stranger to police attentions. A local lawyer who had become immensely, and mysteriously, rich, he was a thin-faced man in his late thirties, dressed immaculately in a dark pinstripe suit with a white handkerchief poking out of its breast pocket. A man who had helped Eddie Gayle wheedle his way out of more than a few tight spots over the years, D'Arcy interested the police greatly. Alerted to the lawyer's wealth by his large house on the western side of the city, and the expensive cars parked on its gravelled drive, detectives had long suspected him of laundering dirty money for organised crime in the city.

But, as with his client, proof was difficult to come by, so the slippery D'Arcy remained at large, determined to grasp every opportunity to increase the pressure on the police and ensure that the detectives did not pry too deeply into his own affairs. Despite his hostile expression now, the solicitor actually welcomed the latest police decision to bring Gayle in for questioning. The lawyer found his client a particularly useful tool; if the police were looking at Gayle, they weren't looking at his lawyer.

'I would like to place on record,' began the lawyer icily, 'that as an upstanding citizen, my client objects most strongly to the way he has been brought to this police station on yet another flimsy pretext.'

'But I thought he liked our little chats,' said Blizzard innocently, glancing at the whirring tape machine; the words would sound OK but the recorder would not pick up the thinness of his smile. 'I know I look forward to them immensely and the lovely letters Eddie writes to the chief constable afterwards, complimenting me on my work.'

'Is my client under arrest?' asked D'Arcy.

'Under arrest? Eddie?' said Blizzard, again feigning innocence. 'Oh, no, no, the very thought of it. No, in his capacity as an upstanding citizen he is here to help us with some inquiries. You are an upstanding citizen, aren't you, Eddie?'

Gayle glared at him but said nothing.

'So why exactly is he here?' asked D'Arcy. 'My client is a very busy man…'

'Yes, well once we get this sorted out, he can go back to beating up people.'

'I resent that!' snarled Gayle, leaping to his feet.

'Sit down,' snapped Blizzard.

The landlord hesitated then looked deep into the ice-blue of the chief inspector's eyes and slumped back onto his chair, where he sat eying the detective balefully.

'So what *is* this about?' asked D'Arcy, angry at the ease with which Blizzard had provoked his client into losing his temper. 'Another pointless fishing expedition, I assume?'

'We are making some preliminary inquiries into the discovery of the body at the old POW camp,' said Blizzard.

'So, it is another fishing expedition,' said the lawyer.

'Yeah, I ain't got nothing to do with that!' exclaimed Gayle.

'I am sure you haven't,' said Blizzard. 'But he was found on land owned by one of your associates, one Henderson Ramage, a farming gentleman of this parish.'

'Is that why we are here?' asked the lawyer incredulously, picking up his shiny black briefcase and pointedly snapping it shut. 'Because of Henderson Ramage? Well, this has nothing whatsoever to do with my client. It sounds like you are desperate, Chief Inspector. As per usual.'

'At this stage, I am just trying to get a picture of what happened on the land,' said Blizzard.

'Then talk to Mr Ramage and don't pester my client with these fatuous questions.'

'Mr Ramage is out of town on business,' said Blizzard. 'So, I am talking to your client first. And I am interested,

Mr D'Arcy, because it seems to me that the name means something to you and your client. Would you care to explain that?'

'We have no comment to make,' said the solicitor.

'Yeah, and I ain't saying nothing,' said Gayle, sitting back in the chair, crossing his arms and staring defiantly at the detectives. 'I hardly know him.'

'Fair enough,' said Blizzard.

The chief inspector looked down and started to flick idly through the brown file on the table. Watched uncomfortably by the landlord as he turned the pages over, Blizzard finally settled on one of them and leaned forward to look closer, seemingly entranced by the contents. The seconds lengthened. The silence was oppressive. Gayle and D'Arcy eyed the file uneasily.

'What is that?' asked the lawyer, unable to contain his curiosity any longer.

'What's what?' replied Blizzard innocently.

'That.' He nodded at the document.

'That?' said Blizzard, looking down as if he had only just noticed its presence. 'Oh, that is a file, Mr D'Arcy. Surely you have seen one before? Your office must be full of them. I believe they are usually made out of some form of card.'

Colley allowed himself a smile.

'Don't mess with me,' said D'Arcy. 'What does it contain?'

'It is the file on your client's associate Garry Horton.'

'I ain't never heard of him,' blustered Gayle, running a hand round his grubby shirt collar as he started to sweat even more.

'Oh, come on,' said Colley, his voice hard-edged as he stared at the little landlord. 'Horton works for you. We all know that.'

Eddie Gayle thought for a moment. Next to him, D'Arcy looked uncertain for the first time in the interview.

D'Arcy and Eddie Gayle did indeed know about Garry Horton.

Horton, a 17-stone bruiser now in his early forties, was an ex-bodybuilder with a long record of violence stretching back to his late teens and who had worked for many years as one of Gayle's enforcers. His reign of fear came to an end when he was jailed for a savage attack carried out in one of Eddie Gayle's bedsits. Two tenants, a couple in their late teens, had complained about the state of their room and threatened to go to the city council when Gayle refused to do anything about it.

Late one night, they received a visit from Horton and another heavy, who was never identified. Although he was never able to prove it, Colley had always privately believed the second attacker that night was Henderson Ramage; the farmer knew Horton from school and they were known to still associate with each other. Despite an ugly atmosphere of intimidation, including veiled threats against himself – one of the reasons Colley shared Blizzard's distaste for Gayle – the sergeant eventually managed to persuade the terrified couple to give evidence after several weeks of delicate negotiations at their hospital bedsides. It was to be the first of several jail sentences for Horton in the years that followed.

'And what is so interesting, of course,' said Blizzard, flicking through the file then glancing at his sergeant, 'was the victims' nationality. German, were they not, David?'

'They were,' said the sergeant. 'Exchange students over from Hamburg.'

'Hey, I've just realised, our victim in the grave was German, too,' said Blizzard, fixing Gayle with a steely glare as he dropped his pretence. 'So, you can see why we are so interested in you. After all, Garry Horton is your heavy, is he not?'

'He doesn't work for me,' blustered Gayle.

'But surely all this is irrelevant, Chief Inspector,' said D'Arcy. 'Even if my client did know this Mr Horton, and we deny that to be the case, I understand Mr Horton is in jail and could not possibly have killed the man you found at the farm.'

'It is a point to consider,' said Blizzard.

'Somewhat of an oversight on your part, I can't help feeling,' added D'Arcy.

He smiled triumphantly at the chief inspector, but it was not a convincing smile, more of an act; long experience had taught him that Blizzard did not make those kinds of mistakes. Colley sat back, enjoying the verbal jousting match and waiting for Blizzard's next move. The chief inspector's features were inscrutable. He would have made a fine poker player, thought Colley, as he did so often in these situations.

'You are absolutely right, Mr D'Arcy, it would indeed be an oversight,' said Blizzard calmly. 'Except our victim was actually murdered fifteen years ago – at just about the time Garry was stomping around the city beating up innocent Germans, oddly enough. At your client's behest, might I add. And, as you well know, Garry Horton was released two weeks ago and now appears to have gone missing. Strange coincidence, is it not?'

The solicitor bit his lip. It was always like this representing Eddie Gayle, he reflected gloomily; you were never quite sure of exactly what he was guilty, you just knew it was something. Adding to D'Arcy's unease was the fact that he knew Horton did indeed work for Gayle. Everyone in the room knew it. Knowing it was part of the game.

'But surely,' said the solicitor, 'the radio said you only found the body at the farm last week. It did not mention anything about fifteen years ago.'

'It must have slipped my mind,' said Blizzard, deadpan. 'But that's when he was killed. You know, now I say it like that, the coincidence really does strike you. What do you think, Sergeant?'

'It certainly makes you think,' said Colley.

Gayle and D'Arcy sat there in silence for a few moments, digesting the information. The landlord, perspiring even more now, glanced hopefully at his lawyer, who was thinking quickly for a way to regain the initiative. Once you let John Blizzard gain the upper hand in interviews, life could become extremely difficult indeed.

'Whatever the truth or otherwise of those statements,' said D'Arcy at last, 'none of this has anything to do with my client.'

'Yeah, I ain't got nothing to do with some dead square-head!' exclaimed the landlord angrily.

'Such a wonderful respect for multi-culturalism in this city,' murmured Blizzard. 'No wonder people regard you as such an upstanding citizen, Eddie.'

'Please, Eddie,' hissed the lawyer. 'Let me handle this.'

'Na, he ain't getting away with saying I attacked them Krauts!' said Gayle angrily. 'He can't prove that!'

'Perhaps I don't need to,' murmured Blizzard.

'Chief Inspector,' said D'Arcy. 'I do not appreciate your little games and I fail to see where this is leading us. As I recall, your sergeant here tried to cynically implicate my client in the terrible attack on those two poor exchange students at the time Mr Horton was arrested, and patently failed to do so.'

'Yeah, funny that,' said Colley. 'Even though it happened in your house, no one living there seemed to know who you were, Eddie. And you such a pillar of the community, too.'

'I have had enough of this,' said the lawyer, standing up with a scrape of his chair. 'And since nothing seems to have changed, we are going to take our leave of you. What's more, I will be writing to your chief constable to protest about the way my client has yet again been harassed.'

'I'm sure you will.'

Blizzard wafted a hand at Colley and watched the sergeant escort them out of the room. As he went, Eddie

Gayle leered and made a writing movement in the air at the chief inspector.

'Make sure your lawyer does the letter, Eddie,' said Blizzard. 'Your spelling is atrocious.'

Gayle glared at him and disappeared into the corridor. The chief inspector walked slowly back to his office and closed the door. He was still there two hours later, contemplating whether it was time to go home as the office clock edged towards seven. Blizzard stared moodily out of the window into the inky blackness of a winter evening, scowling as the rain started to fleck against the glass. With a sigh, he glanced back down onto the desk, where Garry Horton's file had laid open for the past thirty minutes. The chief inspector's reverie was disturbed by Colley, who entered clutching a piece of paper.

'Penny for your thoughts?' said the sergeant, perching on the edge of the desk and noticing the far-away expression on Blizzard's face.

'Not sure I have any at this stage.'

'Do you really think Knoefler is a racist murder?'

'No, not really. And let's hope it isn't, we'd have every civil rights campaigner in Hafton besieging the station if it was. Not to mention that silly woman from the diversity relations department or whatever they call it. Agatha Fish-tank or something.'

'Agnetha Flitcroft,' said Colley. 'She's Swedish.'

'Whatever,' grunted Blizzard. 'You know the one I mean, the bimbo with the blonde hair and the three-feet heels.'

'You've always been so politically correct. I bet Danny Wheatley would never say something like that.'

'He'd be too busy counting bollards,' grunted Blizzard. He recalled once again, as he had many times in recent days, his strange experience at the graveside. 'Besides, this goes beyond Eddie Gayle and his hired thugs, I am sure of it. There is something much deeper to this, David, and the answer lies at Green Meadow Farm.'

'This place has really got to you, hasn't it?' said Colley.

Blizzard did not comment and they both listened to the increasingly insistent drumming of the rain on the office window. Colley eyed his friend for a moment.

'What?' asked Blizzard, noticing the look.

'Are you finally going to tell me what spooked you at the graveside?'

'No.'

'I've never seen you like that.'

'You live and learn,' said Blizzard.

The tone of his reply suggested it was a closed matter.

'OK, OK, I get the message,' said Colley. He knew Blizzard would open up to him in time.

The chief inspector looked at the piece of paper in the sergeant's hand.

'What's that?' he asked.

'It's a fax from the German Embassy,' said Colley, handing it over. 'I told you they'd come through. Vorsprung durch Technik and all that.'

'I didn't know you could speak German,' said Blizzard.

'I had an Audi once.'

'Do they know much about Knoefler?' asked the chief inspector.

'Na, they just make cars,' said Colley, trying not to laugh.

'I mean,' said Blizzard, 'the embassy?'

'A bit, not much, mind.'

'Well, whatever it is,' said Blizzard, who never wasted an opportunity to press the case for better computerised systems at Abbey Road, 'it's bound to be a damned site more than our records department would ever dredge up. If it was down to them, it would take us another four years to even find out where bloody Germany is. Now, if we had that new system like they've got over at…'

He scanned the fax. According to the Embassy, Knoefler had indeed been a prisoner-of-war at Hafton

Camp, one of the last POWs to be released just before the complex closed in the middle of 1946: it had stayed open for almost a year after the end of the war. He married an English woman from Hafton a year or so later and they moved to Wales, where Knoefler concentrated all his energies on building up a successful agricultural supplies company which, as the years passed, went into land ownership as well, snapping up considerable acreage in Wales and South-West England from farmers and selling it to housebuilders wishing to expand.

It all made Horst Knoefler a wealthy man and, the couple having not had children to inherit the business, he sold the company in a multi-million-pound deal and he and his wife settled into comfortable retirement in a large house in a remote village in the Welsh countryside. According to the embassy, the last they heard of Knoefler was fifteen years previously when he told them that his wife had died of a heart attack. Grief-stricken, the retired businessman sold their house and promised to inform embassy officials of his new address. He failed to do so and attempts to track him down over the subsequent years had drawn a blank.

'So where did he go after selling the house?' asked Blizzard, putting the piece of paper down on his desk. 'David, have you still got that Taffy mate?'

'Sure have, although how Agatha Fish-tank would react if she heard you calling him that is open to debate.'

'Oh, dear, what a pity. Anyway, get onto him will you, see if he can find out anything about our Herr Knoefler.'

'Ahead of you on that one, guv. Just come off the phone with Jonathan. He contacted a friend of his in the village where Knoefler lived. It's a tiny place, only ten or twenty houses. Turns out the guy just disappeared one day. Never even said his goodbyes, which was unlike him, apparently.'

'Yeah?'

'The locals reckoned he was a polite and courteous guy. Always stopped to say good morning to people on his way to the shop to buy a newspaper, that sort of thing. Everyone liked him.'

'So, Knoefler just upped sticks and left, eh?'

'The villagers never saw hide nor hair of him again. A young couple live in the house now.'

'No police investigation?'

'There didn't seem a need and no one reported him missing.'

'We need to find out who he was running from.'

'If he was running, guv,' cautioned the sergeant. 'Lots of people sell their homes after their partner dies. Can't live with the memories. My nan did that. Saw grandad everywhere. Got too much for her in the end – he was getting in her way, she said – so she sold up.'

'No, Knoefler was running scared. A bloke who always let the embassy know where he was, suddenly disappearing off the face of the earth without so much as a by-your-leave? No, that would have offended his sense of German efficiency.'

'Maybe.'

'Definitely, David,' insisted the chief inspector. 'I am telling you, it was not his style. Besides, look what happens next, he gets himself killed. That's too much of a coincidence. The events have got to be linked.'

'OK, but if they are, where does it leave dearest Eddie Gayle and Henderson Ramage?'

'Not sure. Maybe it leaves them nowhere but, involved or not, it's nice to remind Eddie and his scumbag lawyer that we are watching him, is it not? I don't like the idea that Eddie can run around the city doing whatever the bloody hell he likes. It's gone on for far too long and I don't care what the chief constable says, it has got to end.'

'Agreed, but his lawyer is going to kick up a fuss again, you know what a reptile D'Arcy is, guv. And the super's not going to like that.'

'Not like what?' asked Ronald, walking into the office and fixing the sergeant with a hawkish expression.

'Whoops,' said Colley. 'Me and my big mouth again.'

Blizzard gave him a pained look.

'I know,' said Ronald. He walked out of the office, his voice floating back down the corridor. 'If I pretend I didn't hear anything, perhaps it will go away and I won't have my flabby ass hauled into the chief's office tomorrow morning to explain why we are harassing Eddie Gayle again. Good night, gentlemen…'

Chapter five

'You do know how to show a girl a good time,' said Fee Ellis.

'I do my best,' said Blizzard, smiling cheerfully at the woman who had transformed his life over the past year.

'It's a bit of mess, though.'

'No, it isn't,' said Blizzard as he scrabbled over the pieces of metal piled along the edge of the dimly-lit corrugated iron shed. 'It's lovely.'

'Whatever,' said Fee, shivering with cold and pulling her thin black leather jacket around her.

As she watched him battling his way across the shed, she marvelled at the hold that its contents had exerted over Blizzard for years. She knew from Colley that the shed had been the chief inspector's secret place, his bolt-hole at times of stress, the place to which he ran when he needed to clear his thoughts. Even though she had been there a number of times, Fee still felt somehow out of place, like she did not belong, like this was his place and she was intruding.

Fee had been the chief inspector's girlfriend for a year. Colley used to say that the only way Blizzard could ever hope to hook up with a woman was if he arrested her.

He was nearly right; twenty-eight years old, Fee had been a police officer for six years. Having graduated from university, she initially served as a uniformed constable for five years, over on the eastern side of the city, showing such promise that she had been seconded to Western Division CID to gain experience as a detective.

The daughter of a retired detective sergeant, with whom Blizzard and Ronald had worked briefly in their early days, Fee had impressed the chief inspector the moment she had walked into the squad room, and not just for her professionalism. Five-foot eight and slim, she had short, slightly waved, blonde hair and a face with soft lines, a face that presented a striking contrast, sometimes suggesting someone cool, collected and unapproachable, at other times a person who was warm and animated. Also, on rare unguarded occasions, it suggested the air of vulnerability felt by a woman trying to survive in the man's world that was Hafton CID. She was also a woman who appreciated, right from her initial attraction to the chief inspector, the difficulties of going out with a man like John Blizzard. Avowedly single and set in his ways, and as hardened a detective as they came, he was a man wedded, colleagues said, to his job.

Dressed tonight in jeans and a purple sweater underneath her jacket, Fee was standing in the presence of John Blizzard's other great love. All officers had their releases from the pressure of the job; Colley was a keen rugby player, Chris Ramsey, one of Western CID's two detective inspectors loved martial arts, Fee was a keen cyclist, and for Blizzard the escape was provided by the Old Lady, a steam locomotive.

His fascination with steam stretched back to a grandfather who was a shedmaster in industrial Yorkshire in the pre-war years and a father who worked for a while as a train driver.

The Old Lady, housed in the shed on wasteland on the edge of the city centre, was more correctly known as the Silver Flyer. Childhood passion reaching deep into adulthood, Blizzard had helped form the Hafton Railway Appreciation Society, a small group of enthusiastic volunteers who restored steam locomotives. He had stumbled across the building while investigating a serious assault some years before, standing in amazement as he scraped off the rust to reveal the locomotive's nameplate. It did not take him long to persuade society members to raise the cash to buy and begin to renovate her.

This night, it was a brief visit to the shed, Blizzard simply checking that the building was secure.

'So what *do* you see in her?' asked Fee. She shook her head as he clambered over a pile of engine parts, edged past the main frame of the locomotive and reached up to check the grimy window at the far side of the building.

'She's beautiful,' said Blizzard. Having found the window secure, he began the tortuous journey back, patting the engine affectionately, then cursing as he barked his shin on the edge of a workbench.

'But she's just a chunk of metal,' said Fee.

'That people can say such things about something so beautiful will forever be a sadness to me,' said Blizzard.

'But she's a rust-bucket,' said Fee, pointing to the locomotive.

'You sound like Colley. He always says that.'

'You can't blame us,' said Fee. 'After all, aren't you a touch old to be playing with trains, Mr Blizzard?'

'Colley says that as well,' replied the chief inspector. 'And he also says that having a love affair with one old boiler should be enough for me.'

'Wait until I get to see that sergeant of yours. Talking of which, is that date OK for dinner at their place?'

'Sure is,' said Blizzard, clambering over the last of the pieces of metal and taking her arm. 'I talked to Colley today. He's playing rugby in the afternoon but says he should be out of casualty by eight. Now come on, I seem to recall promising you a drink.'

'You did,' she said, pushing open the creaking door and walking into the sharp chill of a winter night, 'and you can tell me all about Eddie Gayle.'

'Why ruin a nice evening?' grunted Blizzard.

He snapped shut the padlock on the door and followed her across the wasteland towards the car, broken glass crunching beneath their feet and the lights of the city centre twinkling in front of them. For Blizzard, who had grown used to making the journey on his own over the years, it was still a source of wonder that he could do so with Fee Ellis. The chief inspector was glad it was dark and she could not see him grinning like a schoolboy.

* * *

An hour later, as the couple settled down in a cosy nook by the roaring fire in Blizzard's village pub, cradling their drinks – he a pint of real ale, she a white wine spritzer – the uniform constable deputed to guard the murder scene at Green Meadow Farm a few miles away was having a much less enjoyable time. Graveyard shift good and proper, he thought morosely. Stamping his feet to keep warm and glancing longingly at the bright lights of the farmhouse a couple of fields away, he occasionally shone his torch into the darkness, watching uneasily as the beam pierced the night and the shadows danced before his eyes.

Nearby, the grave lay still, silent and empty. The forensics team that had spent most of the day sifting through the cloying soil in the hope of unearthing further evidence had departed as dusk fell, leaving a single officer to stand guard. Now, the constable, who had taken over the watch from his colleague an hour previously, sat down on a small chair at the edge of the grave, greatcoat pulled tightly around him, cup of coffee from his flask warming his hands, and cursed his luck. Periodically, he glanced down at the luminous hands of his watch, praying for midnight to come around quickly so he could be relieved and flee to the relative warmth of Abbey Road Police

Station. Even though the heating system had broken down again late that afternoon it would still be more pleasant than the field.

The constable's unease had not been helped by the stories circulating round the station, spread by other officers who had done the duty and reported how eerie the whole experience had proved. This was the constable's first time at the farm and he was not sure if they were being genuine or had been winding him up. A light breeze blew up and the nearby copse rustled and sighed, and as the officer peered into the darkness, he could have sworn he saw a figure move among the shadowy trees. But just for a moment. Then it was gone. If it were ever there. The constable shook his head and tried to ignore the prickling down his spine. It would be a long enough night without spooking himself with fanciful thoughts, he told himself as he took another sip of coffee.

And yet as he sat, the ghosts of the sixteen dead men seemed to bear down heavily upon him and he felt as if he were being watched. There was indeed something strange about this place, the constable reflected nervously. He was not sure where the words came from but they reverberated in his head. *At the going down of the sun and in the morning, we will remember them.* And in that moment, the constable did just that.

Chapter six

Henderson Ramage did not speak as he sat in the interview room at Abbey Road Police Station. He was a burly man, the face fleshy and jowly, the nose slightly bent after one drunken altercation too many and the teeth yellowing and crooked. His hair, black and lank, did not look like it had been washed for a while and he had not shaved, his chin covered in black stubble. Dressed in a tattered green jumper, brown cords covered in mud-flecks and workmen's boots caked in dried soil, he sat glowering across the table at the detectives.

Like Eddie Gayle, Henderson Ramage was a thug, but locking him up for a long stretch had proved to be beyond the abilities of the many frustrated police officers who had investigated him down the years. Blizzard and Colley sat eying the farmer with ill-disguised contempt.

Sitting next to Ramage was Edward Elsden, his lawyer, a thin well-dressed man whose smart dark suit, blue silk tie and beautifully coiffured, if greying, hair were in sharp contrast to his scruffy client. The lawyer shuffled slightly in his seat, seemingly a trifle embarrassed at Ramage's unkempt appearance.

'So, Henderson,' said a shirt-sleeved Blizzard wearily. 'Let's go through it again, shall we?'

'My client has nothing further to add,' said the lawyer.

'I'm getting sick of this,' said the chief inspector.

* * *

It was approaching 2pm and they had been in the interview room for just over an hour. It had been a thoroughly dispiriting experience for Blizzard and Colley. Ramage had been picked up by Detective Inspector Graham Ross who, as he was leaving Green Meadow Farm that morning, noted a battered white pick-up edging its way along the track. Ramage looked for a moment as if he would turn and flee but thought better of it and surrendered himself to police custody without a struggle. Ramage's ensuing silence continued a frustrating day. Before the two detectives went into the interview, Ross reported that his forensics team had found little of practical use at the graveside. Adding to Blizzard's irritation was the news from Colley that all attempts to track down a relative of Horst Knoefler had also proved fruitless. Further increasing his gloom was Colley's conversation that morning with the tenant farmer at Green Meadow, a fresh-faced pleasant young man called Robin Harvey. Not long out of university when he took over and keen to try out some of his new ideas on agricultural practice, Harvey lived at the farmhouse with his wife and two small children. But Colley's instincts told him ever more strongly that he was not involved.

'Frankly,' said Elsden, 'I really cannot see why we need to go over old ground. My client has already stated that this matter does not concern him, Chief Inspector. He is a simple farmer.'

'Simple farmer, my foot! Your client is as bent as they come and we all know it, Mr Elsden. I very much doubt if he spends much time milking cows.'

'That may be so. He freely admits to less interest in the profession than his father exhibited. Nevertheless, he does acknowledge his responsibilities in the area and assiduously oversees the running of his farm at Burniston by his manager…'

'Oversees the storage of stolen goods, more like,' said Blizzard, flicking idly through Ramage's file on the desk.

'That was many years ago,' replied the lawyer.

'Maybe. Why was your client visiting Green Meadow Farm when he was apprehended by my officers this morning?'

'My client takes a keen interest in the running of Green Meadow Farm and visits periodically to check that all is well with Mr Harvey and his family.'

'I'll bet he does. So where has he been over the past few days?'

'As I have already informed you,' said the lawyer. 'Mr Ramage was out of the area on a business trip.'

'Yes, but he won't sodding well tell us what kind of business will he?' said Blizzard.

'It was legitimate farm business,' said the lawyer. 'Is that not right, Mr Ramage?'

'Yeah,' said the farmer. 'It was.'

'So what was it?' asked Blizzard. 'Because I am damned sure he was not out buying cabbage seed.'

'My client does not feel that he wishes to enlighten you as to its nature.'

'Well, I think he was up to no good,' said Blizzard. 'And I think it is too much of a coincidence that he does his vanishing act just as the JCB turfs up the skeletons on his farm.'

'You can be assured that my client's movements are nothing to do with the matters on which we have been speaking.'

'How can I be assured of anything if he won't tell me where he was or what he was doing?' snapped Blizzard.

'Whatever he was doing, my client does not, as far as he can recall, make a habit of dropping dead Germans into holes in his fields, Chief Inspector,' said Elsden with the wisp of a smile. 'It does so scare the livestock and my client cannot see why you are interested in him in relation to the events at Green Meadow Farm.'

'Because he sodding well owns it!' exclaimed Blizzard.

'Anybody could have trespassed on his lands to deposit the unfortunate Mr Knoefler in the grave.'

'Yeah,' said Ramage. 'There's some real wierdos around.'

'I'll bear that in mind,' grunted Blizzard.

There was a knock on the door. The chief inspector nodded at Colley and the sergeant walked out into the corridor to find an excited Ross. After a hurried conversation, Colley nodded and returned to the room. Ramage watched him sit down but could read nothing from his non-committal expression. Even the lawyer seemed a touch concerned at his demeanour and Blizzard raised a quizzical eyebrow.

'May I?' asked Colley, nodding at Ramage.

'Be my guest,' said Blizzard, gesturing with his hand.

'Henderson,' said Colley with an affable smile. 'Tell me about the little get-togethers in Hut 23.'

Ramage started slightly and his lawyer looked at him. Ramage's confusion was but momentary, and within seconds his face had regained its surly expression, but it was enough for the sergeant. His job was to spot chinks in armour.

'I am waiting,' said Colley.

'I don't know what you are talking about,' said Ramage, the first time he had looked uncomfortable. 'Honest I don't, Mr Colley.'

'I think perhaps you had better start enlightening us,' said Blizzard, uncomfortably aware that he did not know what his sergeant was talking about either.

'I think there has been more going on at Green Meadow Farm than our Mr Ramage has been letting on,' said the sergeant. He turned to Blizzard with a mischievous look. 'How do you fancy a little trip out?'

'You're the boss,' said the bemused detective.

'Excellent,' said Colley, standing up with a scrape of the chair. 'Then might I suggest your root out your wellies.'

Chapter seven

The memories hung thick as cobwebs in Hut 23. And there were plenty of cobwebs in Hut 23. Standing wrinkling his nose in the musty atmosphere created by a mixture of dust and decay, tinged with decades of old engine oil and rotted animal feed, John Blizzard felt the memories strongly even though they were not his. Felt the presence of those who had gone, heard their voices and the song and banter of comradeship. Felt he knew the men who had once lived out their lives within the hut's walls, could see them reading, playing cards or writing letters home in the dim light. It was a strange feeling, like he was standing to one side, allowed a tantalising glimpse into the past. Like everything was being played to him as if it were on black-and-white film; a film to which he knew only part of the ending. Knew that its participants now lay cold and silent in Peter Reynolds' mortuary at the city hospital.

And always Blizzard felt the man's presence, stronger than before. Knew now why the events at the farm had so disturbed him. Knew what this was all about. Knew who it was about. Had known from the start. Knew why it was happening and why he felt these unfamiliar feelings. It was to do with what the Americans called 'closure'. Blizzard hated the word but had nevertheless felt that same need ever since he realised that he was on the road to fifty. The realisation, coupled with the death from cancer of two old school friends over the past two years and laced with his constant awareness that he was much older than Fee, had imbued the chief inspector with a sense of mortality for the first time in his life. It was a strange feeling, a sensation that somehow Fee had given him a reason to live that he did not have before, and had given him a desire to tidy up some loose ends. The man was a loose end, and in some way Blizzard could not yet understand, Hafton POW Camp was part of his story.

Not that Blizzard was about to divulge any of his thoughts in public. These were private thoughts and not even Fee, nor Colley, had been privy to them although both had noted the pronounced changes in his demeanour since the bodies were found, and had asked him about it at different times over the past few days. Even a concerned Arthur Ronald had asked him if he was alright but Blizzard had said nothing, even though he was uncomfortably aware of the change in himself, too. For a man who had long prided himself on a single-minded, hard-headed approach to the job, such considerations were disturbing and even frightening. And distracting. And he did not like being distracted.

Hut 23 stood at the furthest end of the camp complex. Reached by beating a muddy path through alder trees and straggly bushes, whose branches had scratched and clawed at the officers' coats and faces, the huts stood silent and empty, some with gaping holes in their sloping roofs, others with windows blackened and cracked. Peering in through one of them as they made their way towards Hut 23, Blizzard could just make out in the gloom crumbling walls with faded murals running along one side. Painted by the German prisoners, they included a rudimentary depiction of a river, the Rhine presumably, and a crude image of poorly drawn cows in green fields.

Images of a home which fifteen of the men would never see again. Maybe Horst Knoefler never saw it either. Who could tell?

In the hut next to number 23, Blizzard saw the remnants of piled-up agricultural sacks and a rusted engine motor and another mural on a far wall, a faded image of Hitler, simply fashioned in black chalk yet sinister for all that, as the Führer stood with his arm raised in the familiar salute. Blizzard, who had spent part of the weekend reading about the camps, knew from the library books that such motifs at POW camps had been banned by the British military; found himself wondering at the mural's survival into the 1990s. Peering through the window, letting the others walk on to Hut 23, he felt there was something very real, very now, about the picture. For all it was a long time since the prisoners lived there, the chief inspector felt as if they had never left. Until the previous week, he reminded himself, fifteen of them hadn't.

Thought of the murdered man brought Blizzard back to the present as, flanked by Ross and Colley, who was looking at him intently, he now stood in Hut 23, the most ramshackle of the lot. Large gashes in the roof had allowed the rain to pour in over the years with the result that the walls were damp and mould-infested and half the timber floorboards had rotted away, creating a hole six feet long and as much wide. The surviving floor was littered with rotted wood and clumps of plaster from the wall and the air was thick with damp; Blizzard could almost feel the spores of mould swirling about him. Realising that the others – Doctor Hamer and Elspeth Roberts – were looking for him to say something, Blizzard dragged himself from his reverie.

'So how did you find it?' he asked Ross, looking down at the hole.

'Once we had done the graves, we started searching the huts,' explained the forensics chief, pointing to the floor. 'And found this.'

Blizzard crouched and peered down. The area beneath the floorboards had been opened out to create what appeared to be a hiding place beneath the remaining timbers. In one corner, not noticeable unless you looked for them, were a couple of duvets, pillows and the remnants of food wrappers and drink cartons. In another corner, deep in the shadows, was an ashtray with a number of stubbed-out butts and several empty beer bottles. Blizzard recognised the brand of beer immediately. One of his favourites. A nice drop.

'Not exactly the kind of things you would expect to be left over from a 1940s wartime camp, Graham,' said Blizzard, glancing at Ross.

'Indeed not. We haven't had chance to do a full examination – thought you would like to see it all first – but it does not take a genius to work out they are modern. I had a glance at one of the bottles. Says the beer was brewed two years ago.'

'So, what is it doing here?'

'Ordinarily, I would have thought it was left by the farmhands,' said Ross. 'But this is the worst of the huts. Huts 1 and 4, for example, have their roofs on and are nice and dry. In fact, we sheltered in them when the rain came on yesterday. If you were going to hunker down and knock back a couple of beers out of sight of the farmhouse, they would be much more comfortable.'

'No, I don't think this is a social thing,' said Blizzard, straightening up and grimacing as his knee emitted a cracking sound. 'No, this is a hiding place sure enough, Graham.'

'I agree,' said Ross.

Blizzard looked at Hamer and Roberts.

'Could this be anything to do with your people? Maybe enjoying a quick snifter?' The chief inspector glanced at the bedding and added slyly, 'Or something else while on duty?'

'No.' Hamer shook his head. 'Definitely not.'

'Not archaeologists' style, eh?' said Blizzard, looking at Elspeth. 'Any explanations, Mrs Roberts?'

Determined not to be shown up this time, she also shook her head.

'No, Chief Inspector,' she said. 'None at all. It is most strange. As your officer here says, Hut 23 is in the worst condition of the lot.'

'How come you did not find the duvet and the other things?' asked Colley, who had been wandering round the hut, occasionally running a hand along its crumbling wall, but had now returned to stare into the hole.

'I am pretty sure they were not there when I last came in here,' said Roberts, a defensive tone in her voice.

'Which was when?' asked Colley.

'Three months ago.'

'Why so long?'

'This is a large job,' she explained. 'Each hut needs to be carefully chronicled and examined.'

'What's to examine?' asked the sergeant.

'When the camp was closed, some of the prisoners left personal possessions behind. We also discovered some fascinating material in one of the offices. That took us several weeks to examine and record. We would not have moved onto a detailed examination of this hut for several weeks.'

'So the stuff was put here sometime in the past three months,' said Blizzard.

'Not necessarily, guv,' said Ross. 'Could have been much longer. The archaeologists could simply have missed it when they first came in here. We only found it because we were looking for things out of the ordinary, remember.'

He paused but could resist the temptation no longer.

'As they say,' he said, starting to laugh, 'police discovered a hole and are looking into it.'

'Your scriptwriter is worse than his,' said Blizzard, gesturing to the grinning Colley.

'Sorry, guv,' said Ross.

'So,' said the chief inspector, allowing the detectives time to enjoy the joke but suddenly serious when he noticed that neither Hamer or Roberts were laughing, 'we have no idea at all when these things were placed there?'

'Not at this stage,' said Ross, covering up his smile.

'We'll be able to narrow it down when we get the stuff back to the lab. Just a pity the archaeologists cannot be more precise.'

'We have been working as fast as we can,' said Elspeth. 'It's not our fault.'

'It really isn't,' said Hamer, also bridling at the comment.

'For God's sake, don't be so bloody defensive!' exclaimed Blizzard. 'I just need to get some answers! I am not blaming anyone. Yet.'

'Elspeth is just saying,' replied Hamer, slightly mollified. 'That we are working in difficult circumstances.'

'We have to, given the situation,' added Roberts.

'You mean us?' asked Blizzard.

'Now who's being defensive?' said Hamer.

Blizzard glared at him.

'Your presence does not exactly help, Chief Inspector,' said Roberts, speaking quickly to head off further confrontation, 'but no, actually, I meant Mr Ramage. He has been most insistent right from the moment the housing plan was put back on the table that we finish as quickly as possible.'

'Has he now?' said the chief inspector. 'Why would he do that?'

'He said the terms of his agreement with the house-builders included a clause that construction work would start in early October or else they had the right to withdraw and he would have to repay the money they paid for the land. Our presence has already delayed that by several.'

'He won't like that,' grunted Blizzard.

'Indeed not,' said Hamer. 'Not surprisingly, the housebuilders are beginning to ask him somewhat pointed questions and our presence here has angered him more and more, I fear. There have been several angry exchanges with him. Goodness knows what he thinks about you.'

'If you want to find out more…' Roberts' voice tailed off and she looked at the floor.

'Go on,' said Blizzard, eying her keenly.

'It's nothing,' she mumbled.

'Mrs Roberts,' said the chief inspector with an edge in his voice, 'I am sure I do not have to remind you that this is a murder investigation.'

'She told me not to say anything,' said Roberts, looking at him unhappily.

'Precisely the reason why you should tell us,' said Blizzard. 'And who, pray, is she?'

'Moira Savage.'

'The chair of the parish council?'

Roberts nodded uncomfortably.

'Where does she fit into this?' asked the chief inspector.

'We have been working together on some research.'

'What kind of research?'

'To do with the camp.'

'What to do with the camp?' asked Blizzard.

'I am saying nothing more,' said Elspeth Roberts. 'Just ask Moira about Henderson Ramage.'

'We will. Have you found out anything about our Herr Knoefler?'

'Very little,' said Roberts, fishing a scrap of paper out of her anorak pocket. 'In fact, it is very strange.'

'Strange?'

'Yes. With most soldiers you can normally trace their war records pretty accurately. For instance, we know that Helmut Haller, the man lying next to him in the grave, joined the Army in 1941. We know he was decorated twice and captured in 1943. We even know that he had, at some point, been wounded by a bullet in the shoulder.'

'There is a fracture on the skeleton,' said Ross. 'Reynolds confirmed it was a bullet wound.'

'And the man on the other side,' continued Robert. 'A Peter Schellinger, was from Dusseldorf. He signed up to a tank regiment in 1942 and was captured in 1943.'

'How do you know all this?' asked Colley.

'They're both mentioned in the material we found in the camp office, which matches with papers we found in the reference library.'

'But nothing like that on Knoefler?' asked Blizzard.

'Nothing,' said Roberts, a perplexed expression on her face as she handed the chief inspector the piece of paper, a photocopy of a handwritten camp record. 'Nothing at all.'

Blizzard screwed up his eyes as he tried to decipher the handwritten scrawl snaking its way across the page.

'You're not wrong,' he commented after a few moments. 'It does seem somewhat sparse.'

'It's all we have,' said Roberts. 'Not that it is of much use, as you can see. It states when he arrived at the camp – mid-1943 – and when he left, but nothing more. No personal information. Not even a home address in Germany. And we have been unable to find out anything about where he spent the war or even which unit he served with. I don't understand it – it is as if Horst Knoefler never existed before he came to Hafton.'

'Perhaps, Mrs Roberts,' said Blizzard as he walked out of the hut into the crisp afternoon air, 'he didn't.'

Chapter eight

The chill in the streets of Hawkwith village late that afternoon was nothing compared to the ice forming in Moira Savage's front room as she sat on the sofa, surveying Blizzard and his sergeant with the kind of expression she might normally reserve for something unpleasant stuck to the bottom of her shoe. In Blizzard's jaundiced view, she typified the village perfectly.

Her home, the imposing White House, set back from the green behind a high fence and with ivy creeping across its walls, smacked of wealth. Blizzard and Colley had arrived at the house as dusk was falling, ringing the bell and waiting for almost a minute for an answer. They shifted uncomfortably from one foot to another in the chilly porch, as if they were being deliberately forced to wait. Eventually, Moira Savage opened the door and eyed them suspiciously, demanding to see their identification and reading every word written on the warrant cards with minute and deliberate interest as she peered above the rim of her metal-framed spectacles.

Then, reluctantly and with a pained sigh, she ushered them into the house, insisting that they take off their shoes at the front door and leading them into a large living room, carpeted in cream and lined with classy ornaments and expensive original paintings. Attempts at small-talk having failed, and the parish council chairwoman having not even offered them a cup of tea, they all sat in silence, the officers perched uncomfortably on the edge of the cream sofa, terrified lest they mark it in some way.

'So, are you going to answer the question?' said Blizzard.

Quite what this pillar of the community was concealing intrigued him. Moira Savage was a well-known and much-respected figure in rural circles, not just chair of Hawkwith Parish Council but a major mover in W.I and W.R.V.S circles and, if some were to be believed, a certainty for the Honours List before long. Having constructed a fearsome reputation for not suffering fools gladly, if at all, she was now giving the very clear impression that the detectives' presence was an unnecessary and unwanted intrusion.

'I will not answer your question unless you tell me who suggested you come here,' said Moira in her cultured voice, the tone overtly hostile as she fixed the detectives with that icy stare again.

Here was a woman who was not going to be intimidated by a couple of police officers, thought Blizzard. He smiled slightly, it was just the kind of challenge he relished, particularly given his innate dislike of the blue rinse brigade and his equally strong distaste for pushy women, a viewpoint that had led to the chief inspector being accused of misogyny on more than a few occasions by frustrated female colleagues, particularly in the HR department at headquarters. But, as Blizzard was at pains to stress to the long-suffering Ronald whenever the complaints arrived, that was a HR thing, not a woman thing.

'I told you,' said Blizzard, 'we do not divulge the names of...'

'I imagine it was that Harry Porter. He's just the kind of busybody that would do that.'

'Please, Mrs Savage.'

'Or that Betsy Palmer. Oh, yes…' The laugh was dry and bitter. 'She would just love to see me dragged off in irons to the police station. Step into my grave that one would.'

'An unfortunate turn of phrase,' murmured Blizzard. 'Besides, we are not here to arrest you. We just want…'

'Or that Elspeth Roberts, I always thought she was the type to…'

'Please, Mrs Savage, all we want is to know about you and Henderson Ramage.'

'I do not wish to discuss that horrible man!'

'Will you just tell us what happened, for God's sake!' exclaimed Blizzard.

The show of emotion seemed to work and, after staring at him for a moment, something in Moira Savage changed and she nodded meekly. Suddenly, there was an air of vulnerability they had not seen in her before and her features softened.

'Would you gentlemen like a cup of tea?' she said. 'This could take some time.'

Ten minutes later, as the detectives sipped from china cups and nibbled at biscuits, the atmosphere in the room had changed completely. Suddenly, Moira Savage looked like she was ready to unburden herself of a dark secret. Whether it was Blizzard's harsh tone of voice, or the realisation that the detectives would find out her secret anyway, Moira Savage had decided to co-operate, a relief to Blizzard, who knew from tough experience that buttoned-up Tory women were the hardest of nuts to crack if they set their minds to it. Give me a mindless thug any day, he thought. You could reason with mindless thugs.

'I apologise if I was a bit short earlier,' said Moira. 'It is just that this affair with the housing development has been somewhat fractious, as you can imagine.'

'But I thought everyone was against it?' asked Colley.

'Not everyone, alas, Sergeant,' said Moira, shaking her head. 'They were the first time it was proposed fifteen years ago but nothing ever happened so we assumed that he had dropped the idea. When the idea was revived, the parish council had a meeting about it. I have to be frank, I was shocked at what transpired. I expected complete support for my motion to oppose the development again but that did not happen this time.'

'Why not?' asked Blizzard.

'The meeting turned into a heated affair and some harsh things were said. Mr Ramage made some highly personal comments about some of the councillors, myself included. In the end, we voted nine to two to oppose his plan. Mr Ramage stormed out, uttering some profanities as he did. It was all very unpleasant.'

'Is there not a touch of irony here, Mrs Savage?' said Blizzard and he looked around him. 'I mean, this house itself is fairly recent, surely?'

'They were different times, Chief Inspector,' said Moira sharply.

'Of course, they were,' said Blizzard, ignoring her frosty look. 'So tell me, what were your reasons for opposing the plan?'

'The village would become too large.' She became animated, 'Besides, the last thing we should be doing is taking away our countryside. Hafton is expanding rapidly enough as it is without losing more land around our villages. And the proposal includes the felling of a number of mature trees, which are habitats for wild birds.'

'Then there's the POW camp,' commented Colley.

'Yes, that as well. Although the housing would in theory skirt round the edge of the camp, we all know what happens – give it a year or so and there would be an application to build more. The only way they could expand the estate would be to bulldoze the huts but I have made no secret of the fact that I think the camp should be preserved.'

'Why?' asked the sergeant.

'I am sure it would make a tourist attraction,' said Moira. 'Perhaps we could expand it to celebrate the history of the Hafton Regiment as well.'

'Can't see it,' said Colley.

'It's an important historical site, David,' said Blizzard. 'There's not many of these places left.'

'I am delighted to hear that you share my beliefs, Chief Inspector,' said Moira.

'So, if this place is so important,' said Colley, 'how come at least two councillors backed Ramage's housing plan?'

'They were the younger ones,' she said. 'They said that it was time the village moved into the 20th Century, said we needed some new blood. Clearly, they do not realise that until people like me and Brian arrived, this village was dying.'

'Brian?' asked the sergeant.

'My husband.'

'So I guess this has not been good for community spirit,' said Blizzard, conscious of the way tensions always ebbed and flowed in the village where he lived; ebbed and flowed in every small community.

'It has not, Chief Inspector,' replied Moira sadly. 'Although I have to say that the issue merely brought to the surface tensions that had been there for some time.'

'I can see that,' said Blizzard. 'But how does all of this impact on our inquiry, Mrs Savage?'

'I imagine whoever suggested you talk to me was referring to the threats, Chief Inspector.'

'Threats?' asked Blizzard, eyes gleaming. 'From Henderson Ramage?'

'Well, I say threats, maybe that is putting it a touch dramatically.'

'What happened?'

'I have always spoken out very strongly against the housing plan and I sent a strongly worded submission to the Government inspector to consider at the original inquiry. A somewhat short man called Baldridge. Ill-fitting suit. Didn't clean his teeth very well. You can tell a lot about a person by the way they clean their teeth.'

'I'll bear that in mind,' said Blizzard.

'Anyway, someone did not like what I said this time around either because…' She paused, surprising them as her self-contained façade crumbled. 'Certain unpleasant things have happened.'

'Things?' asked Blizzard.

'Yes, one week a pick-up truck was parked across our drive for two or three days running, blocking us in. We could not get the car out and it caused a lot of problems. My husband attends a lot of meetings. He had to use…' She paused for a moment as if about to reveal a terrible and sordid secret. 'Taxis.'

'How terrible,' murmured Blizzard, earning himself a stern look over her spectacles. 'What is the world coming to?'

'And you believe it was Mr Ramage's truck?' asked Colley quickly, trying to avoid one of Blizzard's rows if at all possible.

'Oh, I know it was,' she said. 'I have seen him driving the filthy thing up to the farm.'

'Anything else happen?'

'Yes, one day I noticed two rather burly men standing on the other side of the green.' She gestured through the window into the gathering gloom. 'By the Post Office. Just staring at the house. They did not do anything but the message was clear. Mr Ramage was trying to intimidate me.'

'And did it work?' asked Colley, doubtful that anything could intimidate this indomitable woman.

'It was certainly disturbing,' she said, voice trembling slightly. 'As were the phone calls.'

'Phone calls?' said Blizzard.

'Yes, late at night. They would start whenever I said something in public about the housing plan and go on for several weeks. Then they would stop. Then I would say something else and they would start again.'

'Do you know who the phone calls were from?'

'Nothing is ever said but I knew. It's Henderson Ramage. He is a truly horrible man. It has all caused tensions within our marriage, I am afraid.'

'Tensions?'

'Yes. A couple of my husband's clients received letters saying that he was under investigation by the police for fraud.'

'What does he do for a living?' asked the sergeant.

'He owns Savage's land agents over in Burniston. The letters suggested that he had been misappropriating funds raised during the sale of land.'

'And I take it he was not under investigation?' asked Blizzard.

'Of course not. But it still caused him a lot of trouble. At least two clients that I know of switched to another firm. After that, my husband said he wanted me to drop my opposition to the housing plan. Said it was costing us money. That's Brian all over.'

'But you did not do as your husband said?' asked Blizzard.

'I can't do that, Chief Inspector,' said Moira. 'I love my husband but to give up on this issue would not be right. Not after so long fighting it.'

'Surely you have made your point, though,' said Colley. 'The plan went back to the council this time around and they approved it. That's the end of it, isn't it?'

'I cannot just let it end at that.' She looked more animated than she had been throughout the entire interview. 'The housing estate will destroy the character of this village and it is my duty as parish council chairwoman to make my views known.'

'So, when was the latest incident?' asked Colley.

'A few days ago. She walked over to an antique bureau in the corner of the room and took out a piece of paper. 'This.'

She handed the paper over to the sergeant. Decorated with a crudely drawn gravestone, it read, 'You will lie where they lay if you do not shut up. R.I.P Miora' in capital letters clipped from a newspaper. Colley noted the misspelling of the name for future reference.

'When did this arrive?' asked the sergeant, handing it to Blizzard.

'The day the news broke about the discovery of the bodies,' she said. 'I told some people in the shop that perhaps the area could be designated an official war grave; I said that if that happened, we might be able to block the housing development.'

'Who did you say this to?' asked the chief inspector. 'Who was in the shop?'

'It doesn't really matter,' she said. 'Word goes round villages like this in minutes. I might as well have put a poster on the church notice board.'

'And have you followed up the idea?' asked Colley.

'Yes, I went to see Elspeth Roberts. I know her quite well now and she has been very supportive of my efforts to preserve the camp. I wanted to see if the idea was feasible. The note,' she gestured to the piece of paper in Blizzard's hand, 'was on the mat when I got back home.'

'And who do you think sent it?' asked the chief inspector.

'I think someone told Henderson Ramage about my comments,' she said. 'But I have no proof that he is behind all this.'

'It's a remarkable coincidence if he isn't,' remarked Blizzard. 'From what we hear, he is indeed increasingly angry at all the delays on the site.'

'He's worried that the housing company will pull out,' said Moira. 'Getting them to do that is the main aim of our campaign.'

'Why on earth did you not come to the police about this when it all started?' asked Blizzard in exasperation, glancing down at the note.

'What could you have done?'

'We would have investigated it.'

'Chief Inspector,' said Moira, voice stronger now, composure fully restored, 'I am a great supporter of the work the police do but on this occasion, I fail to see what contacting you would have achieved.'

'Mrs Savage,' said Blizzard earnestly. 'People like Henderson Ramage rely on victims not contacting the police. You should have come to see us.'

'Yes, well there was a reason that I didn't.' The vulnerability was back again as she turned haunted eyes on the detectives.

'Which was?' asked Blizzard.

'I am frightened, Mr Blizzard.' She seemed close to tears. 'I know that Henderson Ramage is an unpleasant man and, if he heard that I had called the police in, who knows what he might have done next? It could only have made things worse.'

'Well, we're in now,' said the chief inspector. 'Like it or not.'

'Yes,' she said, 'I imagine you are.'

* * *

A few minutes later, the officers were walking to the car when Blizzard's mobile phone rang. He listened for a few moments, watched by Colley, then punched the air.

'Yes,' he breathed. 'Oh, yes.'

'You on a promise?' asked Colley.

'No, even better than that,' said Blizzard. 'That was my contact at the city council, the rail company has agreed to sell them Tenby Street Station so they can turn it into a railway museum.'

'And am I pleased about this?' asked Colley, thinking of the dilapidated building a couple of miles outside the city centre.

'It's marvellous,' said Blizzard. 'We can move the Old Lady there.'

'Whatever,' said Colley, who had never understood the chief inspector's passion for railways. 'Personally, I would have thought being on a promise from young Fee was more exciting.'

'Well that just shows you what…' Blizzard paused and looked at his sergeant thoughtfully. 'No, actually you're right, maybe I'll swing round her place later.'

'That's my boy,' said Colley.

Chapter nine

'Perhaps they aren't going to come,' said Blizzard into the darkness.

'They'll come,' replied Fee Ellis from the back seat of the car, but her voice did not sound as confident as earlier in the evening.

'I hope so,' grunted Colley. He shifted uncomfortably in the front passenger seat next to Blizzard. 'I'm missing the eighteenth repeat of Prisoner Cell Block H for this.'

Ellis leaned forward and cuffed him affectionately on the head.

It was midnight, a week after the interview with Moira Savage, and the three officers had been sitting in Blizzard's car, parked in the shadows at Hafton's ferry terminal for the best part of two hours. Stretching out in front of them, the quayside was virtually deserted, illuminated by harsh spotlights, the tarmac glistening from the drizzle that had fallen steadily throughout the evening. A hundred metres to the car's right was the ugly concrete control tower and they could see through the top floor windows a couple of figures moving about in the half-light as they scanned the river for the approach of the ferry.

Beyond the tower, the officers could just make out the dark waters of the River Haft and the glinting reflections of the sprawling chemical complex on the south side, pinpricks of light on a winter's night. To the officers' left, over towards the main road into Hafton city centre, and on a slight rise, was the ferry terminal car park but there were only a few vehicles waiting, barely visible through the border of bedraggled bushes, their occupants concealed by the shadows thrown by the wan street lamps. All in all, it made for a damp and dismal sight.

But the reason the officers were there was far from dismal, promising a glittering prize at the end of the night. A tip-off from one of Ellis's informants had led to a hurriedly-organised joint police and customs operation that promised to deal a major blow against one of the city's most troubling new crime trends. Over recent months, officers had noticed a growing number of men hanging around street corners in bedsit-land, unkempt, thin and emaciated individuals, dressed in ill-fitting jeans and T-shirts and giving the appearance of not having washed for days. That they were illegal immigrants was easy to prove, brought over to Britain from North Africa with no jobs to go to and no visible means of support. There was also growing evidence that they were largely responsible for the worrying rising tide of street robberies in the city.

Detectives surmised that the robbers were either stealing to survive, or to order for the gang who had smuggled them into Britain and Arthur Ronald had made it clear that he wanted the situation brought back under control.

The tip-off that brought Blizzard and his officers to the ferry terminal came from a man who worked on the docks and who seemed truly terrified when he passed the information on to Ellis when they met in a local park the day before. According to the man, a lorry was due to travel over on the last ferry that night, ostensibly carrying a cargo of fruit bound for the local indoor market but really transporting a group of illegal immigrants being smuggled into the UK.

It was more than enough to tantalise Ronald and Blizzard and they moved quickly. Protocol in such situations dictated that customs take the lead, but Ronald had a good relationship with his counterpart at the ferry terminal – Gerry Hope was a former police sergeant – and they quickly agreed to mount a joint operation. So now, dotted around the deserted terminal, were ten customs officers as well as cars containing police. Parked further back, concealed behind sheds next to the main road entrance, were the firearms and tactical support units to be deployed in case of emergency. Ronald and Blizzard had insisted they be there: in one of the incidents, a street robber had produced a handgun when challenged by a member of the public.

During their long vigil in the car, Blizzard had hardly said a word even though Colley and Ellis had made occasional attempts to start conversations. Although seemingly wrapped up in his own thoughts, Blizzard welcomed the action because in the week after the gathering in Hut 23, progress had been slow on the Knoefler inquiry and he was coming under pressure from Ronald to produce a breakthrough. It had all been very frustrating, so Blizzard was praying that the operation at the terminal produced something to deflect the questions away from him especially as enquiries had failed to link anyone else to the death.

* * *

'What's that?' asked Colley, as he scanned the river and noticed a glow in the distance.

'That,' said Blizzard, as the gigantic column of light edged its way round a bend in the river, 'is the ferry, my boy. So, Fee, you still reckon our little friends are on board?'

'My informant seemed pretty convinced,' she said.

'I just hope we don't open it to reveal a truck load of baked beans,' grunted the chief inspector.

The radio crackled. It was Ronald, who was sitting in another car parked on the other side of the quayside, Gerry Hope alongside him. The men, who had worked together over on the Eastern side when Hope was a police officer, had been yarning about the old days and had not, at first, noticed the ferry come into view.

'You see it?' said a disembodied voice.

'We've got it, Arthur,' said Blizzard, watching as the ferry turned towards the terminal.

'Remember, let the customs boys take the lead. They'll watch the lorry off the ferry and do what appears to be a routine search. We don't want to spook anyone. Once they find the illegals, we move in.'

'You can hold our coats' they heard Hope say in the background.

'And your handbags,' said Blizzard.

They heard Hope's laughter over the airwaves. A few minutes later, the ferry was nudging its way into the terminal and the officers could see that for all its blazing lights, there were very few people on board. After it docked, they watched the small number of pedestrians straggle their way down the gangplank with their bags, then turned their attention to the vehicle bay door that was being slowly lowered. A few cars drove down the ramp and across the quayside followed by a couple of lorries, the second of which caught the officer's attention immediately. It was a large blue artic with German lettering on its mud-spattered side.

They watched the vehicle slowly rumble its way down the ramp. Gerry Hope had already checked with the captain of the ferry and confirmed that the vehicle had been registered in Hamburg and the detectives watched with interest as it edged out onto the tarmac and started moving towards them. Two of Hope's officers moved in calmly, one of them holding up a hand and instructing the vehicle to draw to a halt. The detectives could see the man lean out of his cab window and a short conversation ensued, after which he jumped down, revealing himself as a tall, lanky man with straggly brown hair. He was dressed in a red and white checked lumberjack's shirt, jeans and scuffed brown boots.

'Recognise him?' asked Blizzard.

'Difficult to see from here,' murmured Colley, screwing up his eyes.

The driver took the customs officers round to the back of the lorry and began to unlock the rear door. All seemed calm. Suddenly, the driver snapped out a hand and caught the customs man full in the face, sending him crashing backwards to sprawl on the tarmac. The lorry driver produced a gun and pointed it at the customs woman, who backed off, holding her hands up.

'Firearms go, go!' roared Blizzard into the radio and turned the key in the ignition, slamming the car into gear.

With a squeal of tyres, the car shot from the shadows – other vehicles did the same from the other side of the quayside – and veered across the tarmac to where the lorry driver had leapt back into his cab, brandishing his weapon at the two customs officers and shouting at them to keep back. With a guttural roar, the lorry engine sputtered into life and the artic set off with a clashing of gears, rocking and rolling as the driver jammed his foot down on the accelerator. As Blizzard's car sped into the lorry's path, a hand emerged from the cab window and to their horror the detectives could see that the artic driver was pointing the gun in their direction.

'Get down!' yelled Blizzard and turned the wheel frantically, sending the car into a wheel-spin as the lorry thundered past them.

Colley was gripping onto the dashboard as the car swerved but Ellis, who was not wearing a seatbelt, was hurled violently sideways, cracking her head against the window and slumping back onto the seat. Blizzard heard her give a grunt of pain but did not have time to react, instead concentrating on zig-zagging behind the lorry that was picking up speed as it thundered towards the terminal entrance, pursued by several other cars. Blizzard revved the engine and with its tyres squealing, brought the car alongside the artic. The driver leaned out and pointed the weapon again. This time, there was a crack and the whine of the bullet as it whistled over their heads and, with a dull smack, embedded itself in a corrugated iron storage shed.

From the entrance of the terminal, a white car appeared, moving at great speed. It juddered to a halt, side-on in the lorry's path, and two officers in full flak gear leapt out and crouched behind the opened front doors, training their weapons on the approaching artic. For a second it appeared as if the lorry would slam into the police car then it veered off to the right, clipping a line of rubbish bins and sending them scattering across the tarmac. In the careering car ten metres behind, the detectives could see that the lorry driver was desperately battling to regain control of the articulated vehicle but, as he steered it once more towards the terminal exit, more armed officers appeared in his path. A single shot from a police weapon rang out, shattering the windscreen and the lorry veered wildly, the driver slumped across the steering wheel. The squealing artic ploughed into the grassy bank just beneath the car park, sending plumes of soil billowing into the air. For a second or two, it teetered on two wheels then all four wheels returned to earth with a crash. The vehicle shook violently and it was over.

Officers were converging from all sides, some in cars, some running, all coming to a halt as the firearms team edged closer, weapons at the ready. One of the team held up a hand to keep the others back while a colleague ripped open the cab door and trained his gun on the driver.

'Someone call an ambulance!' he shouted.

Other firearm officers edged round to the back of the lorry. A dazed Fee Ellis staggered out of the car and joined the other officers, leaning on Colley's arm as she tried desperately to regain her bearings. One of the firearms officers tentatively lowered the rear door of the artic. As his torch beam illuminated the inside, everyone could see, badly shaken after the collision, a dozen or so men cowering behind fruit crates. They were holding their hands up but the cautious firearms officers kept their weapons trained on them as they were led out one by one. Searches revealed none of the stowaways had weapons and the firearms inspector nodded at Ronald.

'All yours, gents,' he said.

'Thank you, Barry,' said the superintendent.

'Well done, Fee, top notch tip-off,' said Colley, slapping her on the back.

'Ow,' she said.

'You OK?' asked the sergeant.

'Yes, just give me a moment or two,' she said.

Followed by Blizzard and Hope, the superintendent approached the group of men who were now standing next to the battered lorry, shivering in the chill night air and eying the police nervously. As the officers surveyed the North Africans, all of whom were desperately thin and dressed in T-shirts and jeans, Blizzard noticed to his amazement that one was different. Standing apart from the main group, he was an elderly white man, dressed in a black jumper and brown trousers, and altogether more composed than his wide-eyed travelling companions. Before Blizzard had time to consider the point further, one of the younger stowaways stepped forward, produced a scrap of paper from his breast pocket, glanced down then looked at Arthur Ronald.

'Mr Garree Horton?' he asked hopefully in broken English.

Chapter ten

'I am delighted you have agreed to talk to us,' said John Blizzard. 'You are the first person we have met who knows what Horst Knoefler is like.'

'Was like,' corrected Edward Cranmer. 'I have not seen him for the best part of seventy years.'

It was the morning after the events at the terminal and, although Abbey Road Police had been swarming with police and customs officers since early on, none of the apprehended men had said anything. Having gratefully left Ronald to deal with the aftermath, Blizzard and Colley were sitting in a neat little living room in one of the terraced houses a matter of minutes from the city centre. The house was situated just off a main road but although outside there was the usual noise and clatter of life, car engines revving, horns honking and buses groaning, the room was quiet, the only noise the gentle hiss of the gas fire and the ticking of a small clock on the mantelpiece.

House-owner Edward Cranmer sat on the pale blue sofa, composed, calm, hands held together on his lap, and waiting for the next comment from the chief inspector. Blizzard was intrigued by him; up until now, Horst Knoefler had been an ephemeral person, a skeleton in a mortuary, a fleeting name scrawled on a prison camp register. Cranmer could, as it were, put flesh on the bones and cast some light on the life of the man whose killer the detectives sought. And, boy, how they needed some light. So far, it had felt like picking their way through pitch darkness.

Cranmer was a thin, lanky man who exuded a sense of fitness despite his advanced years. Like his house, he was neat and tidy. His thinning white hair was combed across his head, the strands, not one of which was out of place, allowing the detectives glimpses of mottling on the top of the skull, and he had shaved fastidiously, as he did every day, his slightly pointed chin smooth and stubble-free. The room mirrored his pride in appearance. The small table in the window was polished and shiny, the flowers fresh and watered, the standard lamp in the corner topped with a dust-free shade, the two armchairs and the sofa vigorously brushed. Blizzard sat in one of the armchairs, Colley in another, and perched on the sofa, next to Cranmer, was Elspeth Roberts, looking as nervous as ever. She had insisted that Cranmer call the police and the detectives were struck by the way she kept cropping up in their inquiries.

There was another man in the room. Leaning against the wall by the door and saying nothing, Tommy Cranmer, the old man's grandson, was a tall, muscular, well-built individual with strong features and a slightly stub nose. Ex-Army, perhaps, mused Colley. And a bodybuilder, maybe. Or, more likely given the misshapen nose and his blue and yellow hooped shirt, a rugby player like the sergeant. Front row, mused the sergeant, none of them had straight noses.

For all his formidable appearance, Tommy seemed affable enough. Although it was not his house, he welcomed the detectives and busied himself in the kitchen, making tea that was served in green flower-patterned tea-cups and bringing in a plate of biscuits.

'I am not sure I can be of much assistance to you,' said the elder Cranmer.

'You may know something that we don't,' said Blizzard. 'Frankly, that would not be difficult. Horst Knoefler is a real mystery man.'

'That's what I told him,' said Elspeth Roberts.

'How do you two know each other?' asked Colley, looking at her.

'I suddenly remembered that we talked right at the start of our excavations,' she said.

Blizzard raised a quizzical eyebrow.

'I wanted to see what the old place looked like after all these years,' explained Edward, his voice firm and confident, belying his years. 'It was not possible to visit before. In fact, I tried once a couple of years ago but the farmer told me to go away. A somewhat coarse man. Threatened to shoot me if I did not get off his land.'

'Sounds just like Henderson Ramage,' grunted Blizzard.

'That was the name,' said the old man. 'Anyway, when I read in the paper that the archaeologists had moved in, I asked if I could go with them one day.'

He smiled at Elspeth Roberts. 'They were kind enough to let me do so.'

'But why would you want to?' asked Blizzard.

'I learned a couple of years ago that I have heart problems, Chief Inspector,' said Cranmer. 'My doctor believes I may not last much longer and there are some things I want to do before I die.'

'But why the camp, of all places?'

'There is something about it, Chief Inspector,' said Cranmer. 'Such an atmospheric place. It draws you back. It has a sense of so many memories, don't you think?'

'It does indeed,' said Blizzard.

'And some of those memories are mine,' added the old man.

'You were a guard at the camp, I think?' asked Blizzard.

'Yes, I was.'

'How come you ended up there?'

'I started off the war in the Hafton Regiment. Such a sad day when they disbanded it a few years ago.'

'So, what happened?' asked the chief inspector.

'It was such a long time ago,' said Cranmer, his eyes adopting a far-away expression. 'Such a long time and yet it is as if it happened only yesterday. I do not know if you are aware of this but The Haftons were one of the first British regiments ashore on D-Day. At Juno.'

Juno. One word, so many memories. Cranmer paused for a moment, transported back to the chaotic scenes on the beach, hearing again the explosions, the incessant rattle of machine guns and the cries of fallen comrades ringing in his ears, and seeing the scenes of carnage re-enacted in front of his eyes as if they were a film, a film which had been replayed time and time again in his quiet moments down the years.

'Terrible. Truly terrible,' he whispered at length. He shook his head and looking at the detectives with dark eyes. 'Such carnage. You can have no idea what it was like. No one can imagine it unless they were there.'

The detectives waited in respectful silence and after a few seconds, Cranmer recovered himself and continued with his story.

'My war did not last long after the landings,' he said. 'I was wounded near Caen.'

And he was back in the theatre of war again. The Allies were pushing inland through France after the successful D-Day landings and the German Army was starting to fall back. For the first time, the men of the Hafton Regiment could sense victory as they began the race for Berlin. Perhaps such a euphoric feeling after so many years of despair bred complacency in the small group of infantrymen advancing down a country lane a few miles from the city of Caen, rifles cradled in their arms. Whatever the reason, within a few chaotic moments, four of them lay dead.

It was a bright sunlight morning, the kind of morning when it was a joy to be alive, particularly after the slaughter on Juno Beach a few days before. Sensing no danger, they were chatting, cracking jokes, not hiding their presence. Perhaps they let their guard down and missed something, perhaps they were just unlucky. Whatever the reason, a rustling in nearby trees and a voice changed everything. An order. Barked. Harsh. The rat-rat-rat of the machine gun, spraying death along the lane, cutting down the men as they ran desperately for cover behind the nearby wall. Regrouping, a brief fire-fight, then the loud explosion as a grenade landed in the Germans' machine gun nest. Fire, body parts, screams. Then silence and the surviving British soldiers advancing slowly along the lane, guns at the ready, peering nervously through the wafting smoke and seeing the ripped and twisted bodies of the Germans. All dead. Young men just like themselves. A few more widows, a few more orphans.

'We lost four men that day,' said Cranmer, his voice trembling slightly. 'Good men.'

He paused for a moment and his grandson walked over and placed an arm around the old man's shoulder. Colley watched this bull of a man comforting his grandfather with such tenderness. Cranmer patted Tommy's hand appreciatively, looked up at his grandson and nodded, then returned his gaze to the detectives.

'I'm sorry,' the pensioner said, his face clouded, anger replacing sorrow. 'It's just that they were friends, Chief Inspector. I went to school with three of them – and I was born on the same day as Reggie Rostron. Our mums were in neighbouring beds down the infirmary.'

Cranmer shook his head.

'I saw all four of them die that day,' he said quietly. 'Absolutely senseless.'

73

'And yourself?' asked Blizzard.

'I took a bullet,' said Cranmer, patting his right shoulder and allowing himself a wry smile. 'Still gives me jip, particularly in winter. Had to give up mountaineering last year. Pity, I'd planned to do K2.'

The detectives smiled at the quip. Tommy chuckled, relieved that his grandfather had regained some of his spirits.

'Then what happened?' asked Blizzard.

'I was taken to the nearest field hospital. They patched me up and shipped me back home to Hafton. Moved back in with my parents, God bless them.'

'He's not telling it all,' said Tommy. 'Typical Grandad. He got mentioned in dispatches for what he did that day.'

'Oh, Tommy, it was nothing…' began the old man.

'It's important,' insisted Tommy and looked at the detectives. 'I served with the Haftons and I know what Grandad did. It's in the regimental history. When the German machine gun opened up, one of his men fell, hit in the leg, and Grandad carried him to safety under fire. That's how he got the bullet in his shoulder. If he had not done what he did, that soldier would have been killed.'

'Geordie would have done the same for me,' said the old man, looking down at the floor.

'You should be proud of what you did, Mr Cranmer,' said Blizzard, the image of the face in the faded black-and-white picture coming to mind again. 'You should always be proud of it.'

'Thank you,' said Cranmer, clearly affected by the chief inspector's words. 'Thank you.'

'So how come you ended up at the camp?' asked Colley.

'My comrades were dying on the frontline,' said Cranmer softly. 'There was no way I could sit back and do nothing. I tried to get back out to France but the doctors said my arm was too badly damaged so I volunteered to be a guard at Hafton POW Camp instead. At least I was doing something useful.'

'What kind of a place was it?' asked Blizzard.

'Like all the others, I suppose,' said Cranmer. 'There were about 600 German prisoners there when I started. Most of them were happy their war had ended. They had lost the stomach for a fight, Chief Inspector. They knew the game was up. We could see it in their eyes. If you ask me, I'm not sure a lot of the ones in the camp wanted to fight in the first place. They were quite content to see out the war at Hafton. Well, most of them, anyway.'

'Most?' asked Blizzard, recalling the crude image of Hitler that he had seen scrawled on the hut wall.

'Yes, one or two who still carried the flag. Rabble-rousers, Nazis, still believed that Hitler would triumph.' He shook his head in disbelief. 'It was obvious to everyone but them that the war was over but they just didn't get the message.'

'What happened to them?' asked Colley.

'They're not the ones in those graves if that's what you're thinking,' replied Cranmer. '*We* didn't do that kind of thing.'

'We know that,' said Colley. 'So, what did happen to the awkward prisoners?'

'They were shipped off to other camps.'

'There were special high-security camps for their type,' said Blizzard, recalling his recent reading on the subject. 'The idea was to keep them away from the rest of the prisoners, stop them fermenting trouble.'

'We never saw them again,' said Cranmer.

'Was Knoefler one of the troublemakers?' asked Blizzard.

'Him?' Cranmer shook his head. 'No, not him. Good as gold, was Horst. Most of them were.'

'How come you remember him?' asked Colley. 'I mean, like you said, there were hundreds of them there.'

'Demon chess player,' said Cranmer. 'I thought I was good but Horst, he was really something. We used to play a lot and I think I only beat him three times. He used to do this devilish move with his bishops and a rook. Got me every time.'

'So, what was he like?' asked Colley. 'I mean, as a man?'

'Quiet chap. Very courteous even though we were on opposing sides. We got on OK. It was the same with most of the prisoners.'

'We are struggling to find out what happened to Horst before he came to the camp. Any ideas where he had been fighting?' asked Colley.

'He never talked about any of that,' said Cranmer. 'I never asked him and he never asked me. Didn't seem to matter. Both our wars were over.'

'Did anything happen at the camp that might explain why he was killed?' asked the chief inspector.

'Not that I can recall.' Cranmer shook his head. 'To be honest, life was all very uneventful, Chief Inspector. Most of them just wanted the war to end and be shipped home to their families. It was not in their interest to cause trouble.'

'And what about before the war? Do you know anything about his life then?'

'Not much,' said Cranmer. 'I think he said he came from Hamburg. Funny, really, whenever I asked him, he changed the subject.'

'Any idea why?' asked Colley.

'Well, there was one thing,' said the old man cautiously.

'Go on,' replied Blizzard as Cranmer paused for a moment.

'Well, you should not speak ill of the dead,' said Cranmer, lowering his voice a touch, almost as if the German could hear him from beyond the grave, 'but I think Horst was a bit of a spiv.'

'Spiv?'

'Yes. You name it, he could get it when he was in the camp,' Cranmer said. 'Horst could get hold of the kind of chocolate I hadn't seen for years. God knows where he got it from. Anyway, one night, just a few weeks before the war ended, we were sitting outside his hut, sharing a cigarette after a game of chess – he'd got the ciggies as well as I recall – and he told me he might be in trouble when he went home.'

'Did he say why?' asked Blizzard.

'Said he was wanted by the police.'

'Now that is interesting,' said the chief inspector. 'Did he say why they were after him?'

'Said he had been selling stuff on the black market. Said he had a lot to be grateful to Adolf Hitler for.'

'What do you think he meant by that?' asked Colley.

'He gave the impression that if it wasn't for the war, he'd probably have been arrested. Joining the army was his way out. When he saw how interested I was in his story, he clammed up. Told me I must not say anything to anyone. It was the only time I saw him looked worried.'

'And did you say anything?'

'No, I didn't.'

'Not even to a commanding officer?' said Blizzard, raising an eyebrow. 'Or the local police?'

'Do you think the police would have been interested in some German black-market racketeer with a neat line in ciggies and bars of chocolate?'

'Plenty of Hafton spivs to worry about,' said the chief inspector.

'Exactly,' said Cranmer. 'Although you would know more about that than I would. Anyway, all I know is that we never spoke of it again.'

'Did you see Horst after the war?' asked Colley.

'No.' The old man shook his head again. 'When it was all over, we went our separate ways. The camp stayed open for a few months after the end of the war but I left and got a job at local engineering factory four or five months before it closed. I never went back.'

'Any idea what happened to Horst when he was released?' asked Blizzard.

'None, I am afraid.'

'You never met up?'

'No. If the truth be told, I felt guilty about how friendly we had been with the POWs. I felt I had let down the lads that died that day near Caen. And all the others. So when the war finished, so did our relationship.'

'But did you not come to think of him as a friend?' asked Colley. 'At least in some way?'

'No,' said the old man, eyes suddenly burning bright, 'not a friend, Sergeant. A human being, yes, but not a friend. It's never really over, you see.'

'It certainly isn't,' murmured Blizzard.

'So how come you did not come forward when we named Horst Knoefler at the press conference?' asked Colley.

'Couldn't see the point, really,' said Cranmer. 'I haven't seen him since the day I left the camp. What use could I be? It was Elspeth here that suggested I contact you.'

'I thought he might know something of use,' she said. 'It took me a while to track his address down. I hope I did the right thing.'

'You did,' said Blizzard. 'Oh, did you find out anything about Moira Savage's idea? Could the camp become an official war grave?'

'I don't really think so,' she said cautiously. 'For a start, I understand several of the families in Germany have already requested that their relatives be shipped home.'

'They have,' said Blizzard. 'But, in theory, it could become a war grave if some of the bodies stayed in Hafton?'

'That would be for others to decide,' she said. 'You think it's a good idea, don't you, Edward?'

'I do actually. Most of them were decent blokes. They deserve a proper resting place. But...' He fixed the detectives with a quizzical expression. 'I am still a bit confused. What on earth could any of this have to do with Horst's death?'

'What indeed?' murmured Blizzard, glancing out of the window and noticing without much surprise that it had started to rain again. 'What indeed?'

They left the house a few minutes later and on their way to the car, Blizzard said, 'I'll drop you off at the factory, there's something I need to do.'

'Not going off on one of your tangents again, are you?' asked Colley suspiciously.

'No, it's nothing to do with the inquiry,' said Blizzard. 'Honest.'

Chapter eleven

An hour later, having dropped Colley off at Abbey Road, Blizzard was standing in the wrecked shell that was Tenby Street Railway Station. Through his passion for local industrial history, Blizzard knew all about the station, which dated back to a time when the growth of the railway in Hafton was rapid, linking the city with the rest of northern England.

The decision to turn it into an unmanned halt took a terrible toll. Tenby Street deteriorated, becoming a target for vandals and arsonists, and its increasingly fragile state meant it was unable to resist the ravages of the harsh northern winters, eventually becoming derelict. That was when the Hafton railway society, led by an appalled John Blizzard, intervened, arguing that the building's historical importance meant it should be preserved. Society members had drawn up a proposal for a railway museum with the Silver Flyer at its heart. Now, Blizzard stood in the musty station, visualising what the loco would look like on the main platform, and waited for the man from the city council to arrive. Glancing around at the platform stained with pigeon droppings, at the deserted and darkened ticket booths and into the shadows of the neglected offices through doors that hung off rusting hinges, he shook his head at the thought of all that history being lost for ever. The scrape of a shoe broke into his reverie and he turned and smiled.

'Malcolm,' he said, extending a hand.

Malcolm Watt shook the hand enthusiastically. A slim, earnest young man, dressed in green chords and a yellow shirt with green tie, he was the council's tourism officer.

'How's it going?' he asked.

'Fine,' said Blizzard, 'especially since the news that the council is going to turn this into a railway museum.'

'Hey, hey, hey, not so fast,' said Watt as they walked along the platform, watched by the beady-eyed pigeons perching on the rusty rafters above. 'It's still just a proposal from my department – well, I say department, there's me and the kettle – and it still has to go to full council.'

'Yeah, but several of the councillors are old railmen. They'll back it, surely?'

'They are and they will,' said Watt, 'but it's not that easy. You know councils, they're always squeezed for cash and we reckon it would cost at least £15m to turn this place around.'

'So, are you saying the railway museum might not go ahead?' asked the chief inspector anxiously.

'I'm saying it's a brilliant idea but sometimes that's not everything. Surely I don't have to tell you, of all people, what politicians are like?'

They had reached the end of the platform and Blizzard stared out over the nearby wasteland, once occupied by terraces of houses that had long since been demolished.

'How are you getting on with Elspeth Roberts?' asked Watt, turning and starting to walk back down the platform.

'You know her?'

'Yeah. Which council officer do you think first realised what old Willy Savage had on his land?'

'You were the one who spoke out about the huts?' asked Blizzard.

'Sure did. Everyone had forgotten about them.'

'So, when did you meet Elspeth?'

'We knew each other at university. I was studying planning and she was doing archaeology. In fact,' he looked slightly embarrassed, 'we even went out a couple of times.'

Blizzard raised a quizzical eyebrow.

'Didn't work, though,' said Watt sadly. 'Anyhow, moving on rapidly, when the university team was called in to survey the camp I rang her up again. Went out for a drink with her.'

'I thought she was married?'

'It was purely platonic. Anyway, that's beside the point. Elspeth is passionate about her work and really keen to see the POW camp saved. She'd do anything in her power to achieve that.'

'And what do you think?' asked Blizzard.

'Actually, I prefer the railway museum idea, but what I think does not come into it.'

'Meaning?'

'Four or five months ago, just after I had got the tourism officer's job, a number of opposition councillors came to see me.'

'What did they want?'

'It was all very hush-hush but they reckoned the camp would make a good tourist attraction and wanted my support in lobbying for the council to spend money on converting it.'

'Why were they suddenly so interested?'

'Several of them were new ones, younger people just elected to the council. A couple of them had relatives who had been in the Hafton Regiment; I think they saw it as a chance to celebrate the history of the Haftons. Oh, and as chance to make a name for themselves.'

'Sounds like Moira Savage got to them,' grunted Blizzard.

'Let's just say she is an energetic and persuasive woman when she has the bit between her teeth. And, like I said, the councillors who came to see me *were* Conservatives. But what I am saying is…'

'I know what you're saying, that you're not sure the council can support the camp and this place.'

'Unfortunately.' Watt looked at the chief inspector apologetically. 'Mind, until all this thing blew up at the farm, the railway museum still had a chance, the last thing Labour was going to do was back anything put forward by the Tories. But the discovery of the bodies put a different spin on it and there are quite a few Labour councillors prepared to entertain the idea now. And, remember, there's an election coming up.'

'So?'

'Celebrating the Hafton Regiment will play well to the electorate.'

'But can't you put a word in for this place?' The chief inspector glanced around him. 'It needs a few friends right now.'

'I will try but you have not got a hell of a lot of friends in city hall. You're not exactly the most diplomatic of men.'

'Politics,' snorted Blizzard.

'I hate it as well,' said Watt, 'but you really should learn to play the game better if you want to get things done.'

When he spoke, John Blizzard was struck by how much he sounded like Arthur Ronald.

Chapter twelve

"Are you OK?' asked Blizzard.

It was early afternoon and having returned to Abbey Road Police Station after his meeting at the railway station, the chief inspector was sitting with Fee Ellis in the deserted CID squad room, waiting for other officers to arrive for a briefing. Blizzard had walked in to see her sitting at her desk, holding her head in her hands. Now looking into her face, which was pale and adorned with a livid black eye, his expression underlined his worry. It also illustrated for him yet again the difficulties of working together. At the time their relationship had started, Ronald had suggested that Ellis be transferred to another department but she protested, desperate not to see her fledgling CID career killed off before it started. Blizzard, who could see both viewpoints, had assured Ronald that they could maintain a professional distance between them at work. Reluctantly, Ronald had relented but the couple knew they were on probation. So far, it had worked well, except for those times when she put her life at risk in the line of duty, as had happened at the ferry terminal the night before.

Blizzard knew that was all part of the job – he had faced down enough men with knives and guns in his time – but it did not make it any easier for him. The first time it struck home was when he heard that she had disarmed a man brandishing a wooden stave during a drugs operation on one of the division's toughest housing estates. Blizzard had tried desperately to appear unconcerned when Colley was telling him about it with great enthusiasm but the chief inspector nevertheless felt his heart pounding. It was not a pleasant experience and coping with it did not get any easier; the demands of policing Western Division did not allow it to get any easier. Now, surveying her black eye and weary expression, Blizzard was feeling that uncomfortable sensation again.

'Perhaps you should go off duty,' he suggested.

'Don't be such a fusspot,' said Ellis with a forced smile. 'I'm perfectly fine as long as I don't nod my head.'

'Why not?' asked the chief inspector.

'It makes a strange rattling noise.'

'Have you seen the doc?'

'I shouldn't worry,' she said. 'My friends have been saying for ages that I must have a screw loose to go out with an old fogey like you. This just proves it.'

He stared at her, not sure whether to be relieved that she was not badly hurt or offended by the comment. When he saw the smile creep over her face, he settled for the pained expression he normally reserved for one of Colley's bad jokes.

'You,' said the detective constable, 'are just too easy to string along, Mr Blizzard. And you worry about me too much.'

'OK, point taken,' he said and gave her arm an affectionate squeeze.

'Eh, eh, eh, he's never that nice to me,' said a voice and they turned to see Colley walking in with a wide grin on his face. 'I normally just have to settle for a quick kiss – and no tongues, mind.'

'A thought that conjures up so many negative images,' replied Blizzard. 'But let's be honest, you are not as attractive as the constable here.'

Ellis blushed but said nothing as, with a murmur of voices, more officers filed into the room and Blizzard switched once again into professional mode, stood up and walked over to the desk at the front of the room. Colley, settling himself down in his customary position in the corner, tipping back on his chair, feet resting on the desk, winked at the chief inspector. Blizzard feigned not to see it.

'So, ladies and gentlemen,' said Blizzard, looking at the gathering expectantly, 'let us start to make some sense of all this.'

There was much to make sense of. It had been a busy day at Abbey Road Police Station and, on his return, the chief inspector had roamed the corridors, seeking out officers and demanding updates. His urgency had communicated itself to the investigators; they knew that the longer they went without breakthroughs in the Knoefler case, the greater the pressure from on high became.

'Gerry,' said Blizzard, looking at the customs chief. 'Please give me some answers.'

Gerry Hope, a burly man with thinning black hair and a black moustache, was sitting at one of the desks. Dressed in a dark suit, he had a slightly dishevelled look. Now with dark bags under his blue eyes after a long night, and precious little sleep, he considered his response.

'OK,' he said at length. 'This is what I think we know after this morning's interviews. Well, maybe interviews is putting it a bit strongly because none of these characters speak English and we have had to wait for interpreters to arrive.'

'Have they told you anything?' asked Blizzard.

'From what we can gather, they all come from North Africa. We think the gang smuggling them is from Germany. Probably Hamburg.'

'Any ID?'

'They had nothing at all on them. No money, nothing.'

'Who is the old guy?' asked Blizzard, recalling the white-haired man he had seen standing next to the lorry the night before.

'That's the superintendent,' quipped Colley as, with impeccable timing, Ronald walked in and looked at them in bemusement as the room erupted in raucous laughter.

'I won't ask,' said Ronald, looking at the grinning faces, dragging up a chair and sitting down next to Blizzard.

'Best not to,' said the chief inspector. 'So who is the old guy, Gerry?'

'No idea. Won't talk to us.'

'OK. So where does Garry Horton fit into it?'

'It seems clear that he was their link in this country,' said Hope. 'That was the name on the piece of paper they had, which serves to strengthen our belief that they are being brought in by a gang based in the city rather than the West Midlands, as we at first thought.'

'It could also explain why Eddie Gayle has been keeping a low profile in recent days,' said Detective Sergeant Dave Tulley, a stocky man with fleshy cheeks and a shock of tousled black hair. 'Given that Horton works for him, it could mean that Eddie Gayle is behind all this.'

'It could indeed,' said Blizzard with a gleam in his eye. 'The last thing any of them wanted was being hauled in again just as a delivery was due. That's presumably why they went to ground.'

'And there is a decent link with Henderson Ramage,' said Graham Ross. 'We are pretty sure that some of the illegals being brought in were being kept at Hut 23 before being shipped out somewhere else. Since Ramage owns

Green Meadow Farm, that puts him in the frame as well – and if Ramage is in the frame then so is Eddie Gayle.'

'Maybe,' said Ronald doubtfully. 'But it's a big step up for Eddie, surely? We have had no indication that he is into people smuggling before, have we? I mean, what if Horton and Ramage are working for someone else on this one?'

'Na,' said Tulley. 'Horton is Gayle's man through and through, sir. He hasn't got the brains to find anyone else.'

'OK, so where is Horton?' asked Ronald.

'Nobody is sure,' said Tulley. He gestured to Ellis. 'We have been checking all his usual haunts but no one has seen him since he got out of the clink. Eddie Gayle seems to have disappeared off the face of the earth as well. And, frankly, there is a lot of ground to cover with just the two of us, particularly, since I reckon the constable here should really take some time off.'

'Why?' asked Blizzard, trying not to sound concerned.

'The rattling of her head is really irritating when you are trying to do the crossword,' said Tulley.

Gentle laughter and an embarrassed smile from Ellis.

'I appreciate the concern,' she said. 'I'm OK. Really I am.'

'OK,' said Blizzard, then turned to DI Ramsey. 'Chris, this inquiry is getting more complicated all the time, how many more officers can you let me have?'

Ramsey pondered. Aged in his early thirties, he was slim and tall with short-cropped brown hair, an angular face, a prominent nose and a thin mouth not particularly given to laughing. He was dressed as immaculately as ever, in a grey suit with a perfectly matching powder blue tie, and black shoes. A conscientious, thorough and precise, if unspectacular, detective, he was the one who drew up the rosters and allocated the manpower. It was a role that suited his methodical mind and one that sometimes brought the pragmatic DI into conflict with Blizzard.

'Not that many, guv,' said Ramsey.

'Come on, Chris,' said Blizzard. 'Not this again.'

'You know the score, guv,' replied Ramsey defensively. 'We've got those ram-raids over on the Larchgrove and those indecent assaults at Hadrian Walk. And an attempted murder over in Raglan Street, the guy who was attacked with the baseball bat. That needs sorting pretty damn quick before his mates escalate things. They're angling for revenge and that area is sensitive enough without something like this getting out of hand. You told me that.'

'Yes, I know but…'

'And we had nine burglaries overnight,' said Ramsey, cutting across the exasperated chief inspector as he got into his stride, 'and you know as well as I do that last month the chief constable publicly pledged that all break-ins would be investigated inside 24 hours. It's difficult enough doing that without losing more officers.'

'Yes, I know but…' began Blizzard again.

'You can have three,' said Ramsey. 'And, frankly, that's stretching it.'

'That all?' asked Blizzard, pursing his lips.

'I can't shit them out of my arse,' snapped Ramsey.

Everyone in the room looked at him with surprise; it took a lot to make Chris Ramsey swear.

'OK, OK, point taken,' said Blizzard. 'Let me have them anyway. Arthur, any chance uniform would lend us a couple of bodies?'

'I can ask, but they're really stretched at the moment. I can have a word with Barry Glenhorn over in East Division, maybe he can let us have a couple of his detectives instead.'

'But will they be sober?' said a sly voice which sounded remarkably like Colley's although when everyone looked at him, his face bore an innocent expression.

'I think,' said Ronald tartly as the chuckles rippled round the room, 'that a little more respect for your colleagues would be in order.'

Then, relenting as he realised that the official line sounded ridiculous in front of the officers, he added. 'Pissed or not.'

'Well, whoever we get,' said Blizzard, 'I want us to spend the next couple of days tapping up every informant we know and let's bring in some of the bad lads. I want to turn the heat up on Gayle and Horton. They've got to be somewhere.'

Hey up, thought Colley, the chief inspector's favourite tree line could not be far away.

'Let's shake some trees and see if they fall out,' said Blizzard, not noticing the small smile on Colley's face, and turning to Tulley. 'You're in charge of organising that. Oh, and can you get onto Hamburg police, see if they know anything about Knoefler.'

'OK, guv, but what am I looking for?'

'Sounds like he might have been a black market racketeer in the dim and distant. Could be something or nothing but worth a look all the same.'

'Right-to, guv. Er, will they speak English?'

'You don't, so it won't be a problem,' said Blizzard, getting a laugh for the comment and turning to the forensics chief. 'Graham, anything else?'

'Yeah, like I said, I am pretty sure that Hut 23 is where the illegals are kept when they come in. A couple of the ones lifted last night had the same fags we found in the hut and we found some of the same beer stacked behind the lorry driver's seat.'

'How is the driver?' asked Ronald.

'He'll live,' said Hope. 'Turns out it was not the bullet that knocked him out but hitting his head on the steering wheel.'

'I know how we feels,' murmured Ellis.

'Shouldn't you be at home, Constable?' asked Ronald, looking at her with concern. 'You did take a hell of a whack.'

'No, I'm fine,' said Ellis and, noticing his doubtful look, added, 'honest, guv. I just wish people would stop asking about my health!'

'Well, if you're sure,' said Ronald.

'I am,' she said.

'So, have we got anything on the driver?' asked Blizzard, turning back to Hope.

'He's called Karl Robinson.'

'I know him,' said Tulley. 'Daft lad, do anything for money. And I did hear that he was working for Eddie Gayle at one point. Running errands, that kind of thing.'

'And we all know Eddie's errands,' said Blizzard grimly.

'It does strengthen the theory that the people-trafficking is organised out of Hafton and that Eddie Gayle is pulling the strings,' commented Ronald, glancing at the chief inspector.

'It does indeed. Tulley, do you think one of your lot can fit in an interview with Robinson as well?' Blizzard asked his sergeant, then glanced at Hope. 'Assuming customs are OK with that?'

'Yeah,' said Hope, flapping a hand in agreement. 'I can always go and search some old dear's bag for illegal shampoo or something.'

'Good,' said Blizzard, turning to the DI. 'Chris, are you and the robbery team still OK working with the customs boys on last night's op?'

'No problem,' said Ramsey.

'Thank you,' said Blizzard, conscious of the need for diplomacy after their spat. 'You're doing some good work there. See if you can link the bunch that came in last night with the gangs doing our street robberies.'

'Right-o, guv.'

'OK,' said Blizzard, 'I think that's about it for now. Get out there and make something happen. Oh, David…'

He glanced at Colley as the other officers stood up and started to make their way out of the room.

'Guv?' said the sergeant, flipping his legs off the desk and walking over to the front of the room.

'What about Moira Savage's story?'

'Seems to check out. Other people in the village confirmed bits of it. Some saw the truck, others heard about the bogus complaint against her husband and Moira told a couple of them about the phone calls.'

'And hubby was not on the rob?'

'Not that we know of, but I'm waiting for some calls back on him.'

'And no link between Henderson Ramage and Brian Savage?'

'We're still checking that as well. One or two interesting leads but nothing definite yet.'

'Well, whoever's behind the threats, Moira has hacked them off big time,' said Blizzard, heading out of the squad room.

'Ramage has got to be the most likely candidate, guv,' said Colley, following him into the corridor. 'Most people I talked to in the village seemed pretty supportive of Moira. Even those who disagreed with her don't look particularly dodgy.'

'Nevertheless,' said Blizzard, 'it does give us an excuse to bring Henderson Ramage in again, does it not? Somehow, I think he has been giving a whole new meaning to farm diversification.'

Chapter thirteen

'Did your family lose anyone in the war, John?' asked Jay Priest, looking at Blizzard.

'All these detectives,' said the chief inspector, nodding at Colley and Fee Ellis with a gentle smile on his face, 'and it takes a teacher to ask the right question.'

'It's dealing with guilty-looking children every day that does it,' said Jay.

'I take it you are referring to Colley,' replied Blizzard.

'Something like that.'

It was shortly before eleven on Saturday evening and they were sitting in the terraced house which Colley had shared for the best part of ten years with his girlfriend, a willowy redhead in her early thirties who taught at one of the city's primary schools. Over previous years, the regular gathering had been a threesome, the couple playing host to the chief inspector every other month, he doing the same on a somewhat more occasional basis. But since the arrival on the scene of Fee Ellis, it had become a foursome and, after the inevitable initial awkwardness the first night they tried it, the arrangement had worked out well, to the relief of all concerned. Jay and Fee quickly became friends –

united in their exasperation at their menfolk – and Blizzard and Colley had always had an easy relationship.

That evening, after eating their meal of pasta – Blizzard loved Italian food – they were sitting in the living room with its pastel shades and rustic prints, the soft light afforded by a couple of table lamps and the flickering fake coal fire. Mellow jazz music was playing quietly in the background and Blizzard was lounging in an armchair, glass of wine in hand, Colley was in another chair with a pint of bitter, and Jay and Fee were sitting on the sofa, sipping port and nibbling at chocolates. For Blizzard, although shoptalk was banned at these nights, the gathering had always played an important part in not just his life but also the investigative process, allowing him an escape from the pressures and frustrations of major inquiries.

And this one had more than its fair share of those. There were still far more questions than answers. Despite the arrival of extra officers to the team, the detectives had not been able to track down Eddie Gayle, Garry Horton or Henderson Ramage, informants suggesting that the men had all vanished in the hours after the ferry terminal operation, possibly leaving the city. Attempts to speed up the process in further interviews with the men apprehended at the ferry terminal had proved fruitless. Not even the eager interpreter had been able to persuade them to speak. As for the old man captured at the same time, he had proved even more intransigent, not scared or intimidated and refusing even to give his name; attempts to identify him had so far come to nothing. As a result, the group had been taken to a Home Office holding centre an hour's drive from Hafton to await deportation, taking their secrets with them.

So it was a downcast John Blizzard that headed for Colley's house that Saturday night. However, three hours and several drinks later he was in a much more relaxed and mellow mood and found himself, to his surprise, ready to talk.

'So, did you lose someone?' asked Jay, repeating the question.

'Yes,' Blizzard said softly, nodding at her, 'yes, we did.'

Now, all eyes were turned on him, sensing that somehow this was the reason for his strange behaviour at the graveside and the cause of his distracted demeanour in the days that had followed. Colley fervently hoped it was, because experience had taught him that a distracted John Blizzard did not think clearly when he was investigating cases. Free his mind of the clutter and the chief inspector honed in like a laser on the salient points. That was why he often went to work on the Old Lady during difficult inquiries, to find peace amid the tangled metal and rusty old tools. And, in Colley's view, something to clear his mind was exactly what was needed now, so he waited and watched his friend intently. And hoped.

'My grandfather,' continued Blizzard. 'On my mother's side.'

The chief inspector stared into the flickering firelight, transported for a moment to stand once more by the graveside at the farm, seeing again, through the swirling mists, the man's face, seeing that crooked smile in the photograph, hearing once more the clatter of battle and the rattle of death. And in those seconds in the cosy living room he felt grief and bereavement and loss as acutely as he had during those first moments at the farm. It was the sensation that had surprised him then and it was the sensation that surprised him now. We will remember them at the going down of the sun and in the morning, he thought. And in that moment, John Blizzard remembered the man. And decided it was time for others to remember him as well.

'Frank William Robinson,' he said, adding with a chuckle, 'Frank 2 they used to call him.'

'Frank 2?' asked Colley.

'Yeah, there was another Frank lived in the village, a couple of months older than my grandfather, so they called them Frank 1 and Frank 2. Daft really, Frank 1 had the brightest red hair you ever had seen, they could not have been more different if they had tried.'

Blizzard stood up and walked out into the hallway, returning a moment later with his wallet, which he opened, producing a crumpled black and white photograph, handling it gently like it was delicate silk which could tear at any moment. Unfolding it carefully, like he had a thousand times over the past year, he showed it to them. The first time anyone outside his family had seen it.

'That's him,' he said.

They looked with fascination at the image of a handsome young man, dressed in soldier's uniform and standing in a summer garden, stared at the dark hair cropped short and immaculately groomed, at the angular and prominent cheekbones and at the laughing eyes. They looked at the smile and suddenly knew why it was a picture which so affected John Blizzard. It was almost as if Frank knew they were looking at him and in that moment, he reached out to each of them down the years. It was an uncanny and powerful feeling.

'What happened?' asked Fee, moving over to kneel by the armchair and reaching across to take his hand.

'His troop ship sank in the Azores in 1942,' said Blizzard. 'He was with the Hafton Regiment at the time. They never found his body.'

'That's awful,' said Jay.

'We can only imagine what Frank's final minutes were like,' said Blizzard. 'Or perhaps it is better that we don't.'

'No wonder you have been acting oddly over the past few days,' said Colley.

'Yeah, sorry about that. It never really bothered me before.'

There was an awkward silence for a moment as Blizzard gathered his thoughts.

'Somehow the grave at the farm has assumed an importance for me. I have gone back a couple of times.' He noticed the sergeant's surprised expression. 'Sorry, David, I should have told you, but I didn't go back because of the case, it's just that in a strange way it makes me feel closer to him.'

And he looked down at Fee with an embarrassed smile.

'Stupid really.'

'No, it's not,' said Fee quietly, squeezing his hand. 'We all need to know where we come from, John.'

'Yes,' said Blizzard quietly, nodding at her and squeezing her hand back. 'Yes, I think we do.'

And he turned away to look into the firelight again. He did not want them to see the tears glistening in his eyes.

Chapter fourteen

His mind cleared by his admissions the night before and his mood significantly lightened by the prospect of a day off, Blizzard sweated off his hangover the next morning on a ten-mile bike ride with Fee. It was the kind of crisp and bright morning when it was a joy to be alive. The ice glistened on the hedgerows and the sun glinted off the tarmac beneath wisps of blue sky that heralded a welcome end to a fortnight in which endless winter days had followed endless winter nights.

As the couple rode through the country lanes surrounding the chief inspector's home, chatting idly about nothing in particular, Blizzard felt his alcohol-induced headache gradually dissipating and his spirits rising for the first time in weeks. That it should happen on a bike would have amazed many that knew him before Fee walked into his life. A year earlier and it would have amazed him as well because for many years the chief inspector had harboured a deep dislike of exercise and regarded those who took part in it with great suspicion.

All that had changed eighteen months before when he hosted a press conference at Abbey Road and was horrified at the photograph that appeared in the newspaper that evening. When Colley pointed it out, Blizzard's feeble attempts to blame the double chin on a trick of the light or a bad camera angle only served to make the chief inspector realise that he had to lose some weight.

Blizzard enjoyed his Sunday morning ride that day, he and Fee chatting comfortably about anything that wasn't linked to policing as they rode along the winding lanes to the west of Hafton, appreciating the unaccustomed warmth as the sun burnt away the mist, sending clouds of steam rising from the road surface. Yet always, behind the idle conversation, Blizzard was thinking about the case and starting to come to some conclusions. Feeling as if somehow a great weight had been removed from his shoulders at Colley's house the night before, he soon found himself in a cheerful mood, and after the bike ride the couple went back to his house, changed and went out for lunch at the village pub. Then they drove into the city, where Blizzard spent a couple of hours with his mother in the residential home, talking properly about Frank.

During his visit, Fee visited a friend, spending the entire time talking about John Blizzard. The couple met up again just after four and went back to Fee's terraced house near the city centre for a light tea, sitting by the fire in her cosy living room as the late afternoon gloom closed in. Then Blizzard went to view the battered body of Moira Savage.

The call from Colley came shortly after six and within twenty minutes, the chief inspector and Ellis were driving through the same roads along which they had cycled that morning, the grim expression on their faces contrasting sharply with the happy smiles of a few hours before. The end to a perfect day, Blizzard thought morosely. But his mind had little time to dwell on such prosaic notions because, as so often happened when murders occurred, he felt himself coming alive. He knew it sounded insensitive, and Blizzard did not expect civilians to understand, but murder brought out the best in him, sharpening his instincts. Instincts that he felt had been dulled over the past fortnight by his preoccupations with his own thoughts.

Now the chief inspector saw things more clearly, perhaps for the first time during the inquiry. Knew now the significance of something Colley had told him the previous Friday so that, even before he arrived at Moira Savage's house, things were slotting into place and he had determined on a course of action.

'I've missed something,' said Blizzard as he manoeuvred the car into the dark country lane leading to Hawkwith.

'What do you mean?' asked Fee, trying to sound casual and conceal her apprehension at what they might find when they got there; the sergeant had said it was bad and the sergeant tended not to exaggerate this kind of thing.

'Something Colley mentioned. I didn't listen hard enough,' said Blizzard.

Driving past the flashing lights of the police cars stationed at the entrance to Hawkwith village, he headed down the narrow road along one side of the green and pulled up outside Moira Savage's house. Leaving Ellis to hook up with Sergeant Tulley a little further along the green, Blizzard edged his way through the crowd of curious villagers that had gathered. Brusquely ignoring their questions and ordering a uniformed constable to move them back from the house, he pushed open the gate and walked up the drive, noticing through the illuminated living room window that Graham Ross was already there, briefing two members of his forensic team. Colley was standing on the doorstep, mobile phone clapped to his ear. Seeing the chief inspector approaching, he ended the call and slipped the phone into his anorak pocket.

'Sorry about this, guv,' he said, walking down the drive to meet him.

'No worries,' said the chief inspector. He nodded at the sergeant's pocket. 'Who was on the phone?'

'Jay.'

'Another dinner ruined, eh,' said Blizzard with a wry smile.

'Something like that.'

'So, what have we got?' asked the chief inspector, following his sergeant into the hallway.

'It's a bit of mess,' said Colley, pushing open the door to the living room.

'Tell me something I don't know,' grunted Blizzard.

He stood and surveyed the scene for a few moments. Colley was not wrong. The chief inspector had seen plenty of deaths in his time but somehow that never made it any easier whenever he was confronted by a new one. There was something about the smell that triggered off instinctive feelings of unease in him; that and the realisation that just a short time before on the very spot where he stood, someone had committed the ultimate act of outrage against a fellow human being. And the death of Moira Savage was more of an outrage than most.

She had been beaten to death in an attack whose level of violence Blizzard had rarely seen. Moira Savage lay on the floor by the mantelpiece, her head having been smashed in with a heavy object. One eye was closed and caked in blood, her nose was split and several of her teeth had been knocked out. The blood had poured down her front, soaking into the once-white blouse and tweed skirt, staining them crimson, and flecking her black shoes. Blood had also spattered the nearby wall, the pattern ranged across the pale floral wallpaper. It had been a truly brutal attack.

'Who found her?' asked the chief inspector, shaking his head.

'A neighbour,' said Colley. 'Called in about half-five to borrow a bottle of milk. Found the front door open. Came in here.'

'And where is hubby?' asked Blizzard pointedly, looking back into the hallway.

'Away for a few days. Some kind of conference in Torquay apparently.'

'How convenient,' murmured Blizzard.

'I take it someone has contacted him?'

'Yeah, one of the neighbours. He's on his way back. Reckons he'll arrive about midnight.'

'That's a lot of turns round the ring road,' said Blizzard sardonically. 'He'll be very dizzy by the time he gets home.'

He turned to the forensics chief, who was crouching by the body and surveying the wounds.

'So, what have we got, Graham?' asked the chief inspector.

'It's a nasty one.'

'That's why he had to go through all that extra training,' grunted Blizzard. 'They have to pass a paper in Stating The Bleeding Obvious before they can work on forensics. You'd get on well with Elspeth Roberts.'

'Sorry, guv,' said Ross, standing up and instinctively running a hand through his beautifully coiffured hair.

'Don't worry, you look lovely,' said Blizzard, scowling at the gesture. 'So, what was she killed with?'

'Not sure. Something heavy.'

'A poker perhaps?' asked the chief inspector, nodding at the hearth. 'There's not one there and these kinds of people always have one for show.'

'Maybe,' said Ross. 'Reynolds will be able to tell us more when he does the post-mortem but whatever it was, I am pretty sure it is not in the house now. We've looked everywhere, haven't we, Dave?'

Colley nodded.

'Then look again,' said Blizzard, turning to the sergeant. 'Anyone see anything?'

'Tulley's doing door-to-door but nothing so far,' said Colley, glancing out of the window and noticing Ellis and the sergeant talking to a small group of villagers on the green.

'Well,' said the chief inspector, walking over to stand next to him and staring sourly at the gathering at the front gate. 'Someone out there must know why someone wanted to kill her. What about those who opposed her in the parish council meetings? Remind me where we got with them on Friday, David.'

'Na, it's none of them,' said Colley. 'No way are they the type to murder her. I mean, one of them was Harold Brown. He's a solicitor, for God's sake.'

'Oh, that's alright then,' said Blizzard. 'But you're right, they're not killers and this is not about them. No, whoever it was, they hated Moira Savage enough to bash her brains out and that means there was more at stake than a little falling out among neighbours. And that means we have to look for the person with the strongest motive.'

'And that means,' said Colley, taking up the train of thought, 'those behind the sale of the land at Green Meadow Farm.'

'And if that is the case,' said Ross, 'Henderson Ramage has got to be in the frame, surely?'

'You know,' said Blizzard, walking out into the hallway, 'I think he just might be. Ah, Mrs Roberts, what a pleasant surprise. You seem to turn up everywhere like a bad penny.'

The archaeologist was standing at the front door, an anxious look on her face.

'She wants to come in, sir,' said the uniformed constable who was keeping guard. 'I told her she couldn't.'

'It's OK,' said the chief inspector. 'Might I suggest we go into the kitchen, Mrs Roberts. It is not very pleasant in the living room.'

They sat down at the kitchen table and Blizzard waited for her to speak. She was very upset and had been crying.

'I just heard,' she said at last.

'How?'

'One of her neighbours rang me. Oh, God, it's terrible!' She broke down in tears.

'I didn't know you were that close,' said Blizzard, slightly puzzled.

'We weren't,' she said, suddenly producing a piece of paper from her anorak pocket. 'But I'm terrified that I am going to be next!'

Blizzard took the paper. Decorated with the same crudely drawn gravestone they had seen in the threatening note sent to Moira Savage, it simply said, in letters snipped from a newspaper: 'I warned you to keep your nose out. RIP, Bitch'.

'You know, Mrs Roberts,' said the chief inspector. 'I think you might just be right.'

Chapter fifteen

'I hope you know what you are doing, John,' said Arthur Ronald as they sat in his office shortly before midnight, sipping mugs of tea and occasionally reaching for digestives from the open packet on the desk.

'You're not sure then?'

'I know Brian Savage from my days in Burniston and he's a decent bloke. Member of the Freemasons, past president of Rotary, that sort of thing.'

'Oh, I'll release him immediately then,' said Blizzard, unable to conceal the mockery in his voice. 'And there was me thinking it was wrong that he's been lying his bloody head off since we lifted him.'

Ronald looked at him unhappily. This was one of those moments where he felt the burden of responsibility at its heaviest. The return of Brian Savage to Hawkwith had placed the officers in an extremely difficult situation. Convinced by his lies that the land agent was implicated in the death of his wife, Blizzard had been arguing vociferously that he should be arrested. Ronald, on the other hand, acutely conscious of how it would play in the media if Savage turned out to be an innocent victim, was more circumspect, particularly since he knew that the chief constable always took a keen interest when fellow Lodge members were in trouble. Ronald sighed; he knew that such considerations tended not to register particularly highly on John Blizzard's radar. If at all. The chief inspector's ability to cut through vested interests was one of the reasons Ronald respected his friend as a detective and at the same time one of the reasons he found working with him so challenging.

'You know I didn't mean it that way,' said Ronald, trying again to reason with the chief inspector. 'I'm just saying, what if he's not guilty?'

'Then he would have to explain his lies.'

'Granted, but what if there is another reason for his misleading his wife? Maybe he's having an affair.'

'It is always a possibility,' said Blizzard. 'She'd be enough to drive any man bonkers.'

'All I'm saying is go easy on him until you are sure. He has just lost his wife.'

'Yeah, but that could be because he killed her,' said Blizzard, noticing Ronald's pained look and holding up his hands, 'OK, OK, we'll make it a nice little chat to start with.'

'Go carefully, John,' warned Ronald. 'I know what your nice little chats are like.'

Blizzard smiled broadly – he loved having a reputation – and heaved himself out of the chair to head for the interview room, where an anxious Brian Savage had been waiting with Colley for several minutes. Walking into the room, the chief inspector looked at the land agent for a moment then sat down behind his desk and, recalling Ronald's words, tried to smile at him. It didn't really work and the smile resembled something more like a grimace, serving only to make Brian Savage look even more worried. Next to him, his lawyer, a smartly-dressed young woman shuffled her file.

'Thank you for coming in, Mr Savage,' said Blizzard, trying to retain a semblance of civility. 'I know this is difficult for you.'

'Can't it wait?' asked the lawyer. 'My client's wife has just been murdered, for goodness' sake.'

'I appreciate that, Miss Hewitt,' said Blizzard, 'but I really do need some questions answered if I am to work out who killed her. The first few hours after a murder are crucial.'

The lawyer said nothing but glanced at Savage, who sat with his head in a whirl of shock and confusion. Having returned to Hawkwith shortly after eleven-thirty, he had been met at the door of his home by a stern-faced Colley, who had informed he would not be allowed in his own house and had taken him immediately to the station. Guided to the interview room and given a cup of tea, Savage had sat for several minutes watching the clock on the wall moving inexorably towards midnight.

Blizzard and Colley were watching him intently. It never failed to amaze them how the oppressive atmosphere of the interview room got to even the most composed of characters. Brian Savage was a man who normally cut an imposing figure but was now battling to retain control. A tall, lean man, he had short, neat hair, still largely brown with only a few flecks of grey even though he was in his mid-sixties. His face was thin with high cheekbones, the eyes green, the nose prominent and the mouth thin with a slight tendency to curl downwards. He was dressed casually, yet smartly, in a tweed jacket, black pullover and dark slacks.

'You see,' said Blizzard, trying to sound as relaxed as he could as he reached out to flick on the tape machine, 'we have been finding out some interesting things about you, Mr Savage.'

The land agent looked at him anxiously. 'Like what?' he asked guardedly in his cultured voice.

'Like there is no conference in Torquay,' said Blizzard, watching for a reaction. 'Well, not unless you count a gathering of midwives and somehow I don't think that's quite your thing, Brian.'

'And what's more,' said Colley, 'your car never left the county.'

Savage suddenly realised the extent of police inquiries into his movements.

'I don't know what you mean,' he said, trying to sound calm but failing dismally.

'Oh, I think you do,' said Blizzard, leaning forward across the desk, voice changing suddenly to razor-wire sharp. 'You see, after your wife was murdered, we put out an APB on your vehicle and one of the traffic lads from southern division recalled seeing your Bentley parked up outside a guest house in Halcrombe for most of the afternoon.'

'He must be mistaken,' said Savage.

'Actually, he wasn't. He's a classic car buff and has been considering buying one. We clearly pay our constables too much. There are not that many Bentleys in this area so he stopped to look at it. Said it was there at 2pm and still there are 6.30 when he came back that way, when you were supposed to be in Torquay. Care to explain that, Mr Savage?'

Savage looked at him with mounting horror.

'There's something else that intrigued us,' said Blizzard, allowing himself a thin smile as he took control of the situation. 'See, over the past few days, the sergeant here has been doing some digging – he's good at that – and he discovered that your company has links with one Henderson Ramage and the sale of his land at Green Meadow Farm.'

'So, we handled the sale,' said Savage, now well and truly rattled. 'So, what?'

'More than handled the sale, surely,' said Colley. 'You and Ramage were partners on this one. In fact, you smoothed the deal with a friend of yours who runs a housebuilding company. As I understand it, your cut was 10 per cent of the not inconsiderable profits.'

'Oh, Jesus,' gasped Savage, the true seriousness of his position hitting him for the first time.

'And then,' said Blizzard. 'Someone in the village threatened to wreck it all, started kicking up a fuss, rallying the locals, speaking out in meetings, firing off letters, even campaigning to make it a war grave so the development was blocked. And this was not any old villager, Mr Savage, this was your wife, the indomitable Moira.'

'And now she's dead,' added Colley. 'Isn't that strange?'

'Mr Savage,' said Blizzard, turning piercing eyes on the perspiring land agent. 'I think it is about time you started telling us what has been happening because from where I am sitting, it looks like you had a pretty strong motive to see Moira dispatched to a better world.'

Savage hesitated for a moment then nodded weakly.

'You'd find out anyway,' he said hoarsely.

'We usually do,' said Blizzard, 'we don't like secrets. I take it your wife did not know about the arrangement with Henderson Ramage?'

'No.' Savage shook his head vigorously. 'We kept the company's name out of it. Moira would have killed me if she found out.'

He paused in horror when he realised what he had said.

'Oh, Jesus,' he said, burying his head in his hands and starting to cry. 'Oh, Jesus, what have I done?'

'I don't know,' said Blizzard. 'What have you done, Mr Savage?'

'I think,' said Miss Hewitt, 'that my client has said too much and I really do need time to...'

'They weren't supposed to kill her,' moaned Savage.

'Who weren't?' asked Blizzard quickly.

'Ramage and his bully boys,' said Savage vehemently, lifting his head and staring hard at Blizzard. 'He's an evil man!'

'He is indeed and you certainly do make strange bedfellows. Why on earth did you go in with him?' asked the chief inspector.

'I really do think...' began the lawyer.

'Well, I really do think your client should talk to us without you clucking on in the background,' snapped Blizzard, silencing the solicitor with a look. 'Now, please answer the question, Mr Savage. Why on earth did you get involved with Henderson Ramage?'

'The business has not been doing as well as everyone thinks,' said Savage after glancing at his lawyer, who nodded at him. 'Land prices have been dropping in this area for several years and more of the farmers are holding off until the market turns. I needed something quick and Henderson Ramage provided it.'

'So, what was the plan? Turn the screws on your wife to scare her off?'

'Something like that,' said Savage weakly, the fight going out of him again. 'I had tried to tell her to drop her campaigning so many times but she wouldn't listen.'

'And she wouldn't be scared off either, would she?'

'She just would not quit,' said Savage. 'That was Moira all over. Said no bully boy would keep her quiet.'

'Well, he has now,' said Blizzard. 'So, what happened? I assume that when she started banging on to anyone who would listen about the idea of a consecrated war grave, that was the final straw for Ramage?'

'He rang me a couple of days ago,' said Savage. 'He was absolutely furious. Said she had to be silenced because the housing company was threatening to pull out and take its money back. I said I would have another word with her but he said he would handle it; told me to invent an excuse to get out of the way.'

'And came round and killed her,' said Blizzard.

'Yes.' The voice was hoarse now, virtually a whisper.

'While you spent the afternoon in a guest house.'

'Yes,' said Savage.

'Why did you take the Bentley?' asked Colley. 'Surely you must have realised someone would have noticed it. It's not exactly low profile, is it?'

'Moira would have thought it odd if I didn't take it to Torquay. I always drive it on long trips and I could not afford to raise her suspicions. I tried to park it round the back of the guest house but someone had dumped a skip there so I had to park it on the front.'

He looked at them helplessly.

'I never thought he would do this,' he said, his voice breaking. 'It's a nightmare.'

'It is indeed,' said Blizzard. He walked from the room and headed along the corridor towards Ronald's office.

'Well?' asked the superintendent as the chief inspector walked in. 'All sorted?'

'Depends what you mean by sorted,' said Blizzard, sitting down heavily in a chair and suddenly feeling very weary. 'Put it this way, there might be a vacancy in Brian Savage's Lodge soon.'

'Brilliant.' Ronald groaned and closed his eyes.

'Hey,' said Blizzard, looking at his friend with mischief in his eyes as if the thought had just occurred to him. 'They might let you in, Arthur.'

'Not after your little performance tonight,' said Ronald. 'Or over the past few years for that matter.'

'Don't worry about it,' said Blizzard, standing up and heading back out of the office. 'I'll nip down to B&Q tomorrow and get you a trowel anyway.'

A gloomy Ronald could hear him chuckling all the way down the dimly-lit corridor on his way back to the interview room.

Chapter sixteen

For Blizzard, driving home from Abbey Road in the early hours of the morning having ensured that Brian Savage was locked up for the night, many things were still unclear as he turned them over in his mind. Each time, he came up against the same basic problem, the link between the killing of Moira Savage and Horst Knoefler. Or rather, the lack of a link. Half of the equation was easy. The chief inspector could understand why Moira Savage had been killed; she was standing in the way of a lucrative bit of business for Henderson Ramage.

Not so easy when it came to Brian Savage, though, because the chief inspector was convinced that he did not mean for his wife to be killed; his shock at her murder was too genuine for that. There was no way that Savage could ever have really thought that Ramage's hired thugs would go that far. In his more generous moments, Blizzard could even convince himself that Henderson Ramage did not mean her to be killed either. It was perfectly feasible to imagine how things might have got out of hand when the heavies arrived at the house.

But Horst Knoefler, how did he fit into things, mused the chief inspector as he left the deserted city streets and headed out towards the village where he lived. Perhaps, and this idea was the one that simply would not be dislodged, he did not fit into things at all. No, thought Blizzard with a shake of the head as he pulled up to his front drive, cut the lights and got out and dragged his black binbags out for the morning collection, the answer lay in the damp soil of Green Meadow Farm. Of that he was sure.

It was the dramatic turn of events an hour's drive inland, as Blizzard was struggling to get to sleep, that cast new light on the case. The event happened at the makeshift holding camp where the illegals apprehended at the ferry terminal were taken after their questioning finished. A former RAF airfield, the site had been appropriated by the Home Office eighteen months previously. The idea was that the centre, with its ageing huts and weed-infested runways, would be the temporary holding place for people awaiting deportation. As Blizzard was dozing fitfully, events were taking a distinctly sinister turn.

It meant another brief night for the chief inspector, the call from Gerry Hope coming shortly before 4.30am. What Hope had to say snapped Blizzard wide awake. Two hours before, a white transit van pulled up on the furthest perimeter of the camp and three men wearing black balaclava masks hacked their way through the high wire fence with industrial cutters. The van slammed through the remainder of the fence and drove at high speed towards the huts where the deportees were being held.

A couple of the soldiers on guard, alerted by the revving of the engine, ran across to intercept the van, which slewed to a halt just metres from them. More gang members leapt out and, having opened fire on the soldiers with sawn-off shotguns, smashed their way into the nearest hut. Clearly waiting for their arrival, the group from the ferry terminal rushed out into the night air. The raiders left the younger men to make their own way out but grabbed the older man and bundled him into the van, which screeched away across the grass and out through the gaping hole in the fence and into the night. It was all over in three minutes, a highly professional operation and one that smacked of organised crime. By the time the local police arrived, they were long gone. Hope rang Blizzard during his journey back from the camp, where he had been summoned to survey the scene, and now, shortly after six, the two men were sitting in the chief inspector's office in a largely deserted Abbey Road Police Station. Outside, all was pitch black, dawn still a long way off and they had settled down with mugs of tea.

'I'm getting too old for this getting up early lark,' muttered Hope, taking a sip and hoping it would banish the thick-headed feeling.

'Me, too,' said Blizzard, glancing up at the office clock.

The office door swung open and in breezed David Colley. He was dressed as immaculately as ever in a dark suit, dark blue tie done up and shoes shiny, in stark contrast to Hope in his crumpled grey jacket and mud-spattered dark trousers and Blizzard in a hurriedly thrown-on suit with an unfastened tie draped round his neck.

'Morning, girls,' said Colley cheerily.

'Is he always like this?' asked Hope.

'Yeah,' grunted Blizzard, glancing at his bright-eyed sergeant. 'I blame the amphetamines.'

'Anyone want a top-up?' said Colley, nodding at their mugs.

He disappeared and they could hear the clink of cups further down the corridor then the sergeant returning, whistling cheerfully.

'Too bloody happy,' growled Hope, fatigue seeping through his bones.

'So,' said Colley, entering the office, slumping in a chair and taking an appreciative sip of tea. 'There's a great big floppy-eared mammal bounding around somewhere, gents.'

'There is indeed,' said Hope, fascinated by the image which of a huge rabbit bouncing across the airfield runway. 'They definitely knew who they were after and where he was.'

'And they only took the old fella?' asked Colley.

'Yeah.'

'By force?'

'No.' Hope shook his head. 'One of the guards said he seemed to know they were coming and that he got into the van voluntarily. Even hugged one of the rescuers.'

'And the other illegals, what happened to them?' asked the sergeant.

'The gang just left them to make their own escape,' said Hope. 'The local cops have got most of them now. Three are missing, that's all. And they won't get far, I don't imagine. But it wasn't about them, I'm sure about that.'

'So, what the hell *is* it about, Gerry?' asked Blizzard, glancing at the unshaven customs man. 'What is so special about the old fella?'

'Well,' said Hope, opening his battered brown briefcase, 'I may be able to shed some light on that. You see, I reckon what happened earlier is something to do with your Knoefler fellow.'

'Really?' Blizzard sat forward with a look of intense interest on his face.

'Could be the link we've been looking for, guv,' said Colley.

'It could indeed,' said Hope, handing over a couple of newspaper cuttings.

Blizzard examined them in silence for a moment or two before handing them to the sergeant and looking at the customs officer quizzically.

'Where did you find them?' asked Blizzard.

'They belonged to the old bloke. After the break-out, we searched the hut and found them hidden in the bedstead. The guards had missed them.'

'How?'

'It's the old metal type where you can screw the top off the legs and he had stuffed them down there. Must have forgotten them in the rush to escape, or perhaps he thought we would never find them.'

'German newspapers,' said Blizzard.

'Yeah,' said Hope. 'The story appeared over there the day after you gave that press conference when you said Horst Knoefler was the man in the grave. And see how the word Hafton has been ringed in red pen on both articles.'

'It's certainly very interesting,' said Blizzard, glancing at his sergeant. 'What do you reckon, David, is our man in the truck a relative of Horst Knoefler?'

'Could be,' said Blizzard.

'Let me enlighten you,' said Hope with a triumphant look on his face, rooting around in his briefcase again, fishing out a piece of paper and winking at Colley. 'I always like to keep the best till last. Sort of a big finale.'

'I always said customs were a bunch of drama queens,' grunted Blizzard.

'It's true,' said Colley, with a mischievous expression on his face, 'he does always say that.'

'Don't be surprised if your bags get searched next time you go to Italy,' said Hope to Blizzard but the detectives knew that he was not annoyed.

'So, what have you got?' asked the chief inspector.

'Well, I was going to talk to you last night but your control room said you were busy with the murder over at Hawkwith.'

'Just a bit,' grunted Blizzard.

'Nice to know someone else is having a shite time.'

'I appreciate the sentiment. What were you going to tell me?'

'I got a fax late yesterday from an old mate of mine,' said Hope. 'Lad called Arnie Bellshaw. We started together over in Eastern Division when I was a copper. Arnie married a German girl and moved over there, works as a detective with the police in Hamburg these days.'

'Well, I hope you got further with him than Tulley did with the people he rang,' said Blizzard morosely. 'They hadn't even heard of Horst Knoefler. So much for German sodding efficiency.'

'I'm not surprised they hadn't,' said Hope.

'What makes you say that?'

'All will become clear. Anyway, I sent Arnie a photograph of our mystery old fella from the truck. He came back to me yesterday after one of his informants recognised the bloke.'

'So, who is he?' asked Blizzard.

'None other than Franz Hasse,' said Hope, handing the fax to the chief inspector.

'The name rings a bell,' said Blizzard.

'Drug trafficker.'

'Of course,' said Blizzard with a low whistle. 'I saw his name on a circular when I was in drugs squad; he operated out of Germany, didn't he?'

'Hamburg,' said Hope.

'Hang on,' said Colley. 'Who is he?'

'Big-time criminal,' said Hope. 'Everyone thought he was long retired but we are still very interested in him, as are Interpol. In fact, everyone will be fighting each other to get their hands on him, old as he may be.'

'Pity you've lost him then,' said Blizzard sardonically.

'Er, yes, indeed,' said Hope, an unhappy look creeping over his face. 'There are still warrants out in half a dozen countries for him. He started out as a black market racketeer in Hamburg.'

'Now that is interesting,' murmured Blizzard, 'because that is exactly what Edward Cranmer said about Horst Knoefler.'

'Yeah, that could well explain a lot,' said Hope. 'Franz appears to have taken over the criminal activities of his older brother, one Martin Hasse. During the war, Martin goes off to do his duty for barmy Adolf but Franz is too young to join up. In the years that follows, he builds up the criminal empire.'

'And not just drugs, as I recall,' said Blizzard.

'Indeed. There were a lot of lads that came out of the army with their weapons and after the war Hasse ran a black market selling their guns to criminal gangs all over Europe. Apparently, he was responsible for a series of nasty armed robberies in Germany as well. Couple of bank tellers and a cop got shot dead during one of them in Hamburg.'

'So, if Horst was really Hasse's brother, it's not surprising that he did not want to go home,' said Colley. 'The last thing he wanted was to be linked to a cop-killer.'

'Indeed,' said Hope. 'Anyhow, eventually Franz Hasse moved into drugs, heroin mainly. Linked up with a couple of Turkish gangs, took out a couple of rival gangs. All nasty stuff, lots of shooting. Got younger lads to do the work but he was pulling the strings.'

'How come no one managed to arrest him?' asked the sergeant.

'According to Arnie, the cops have been close to him a few times.'

'I can think of someone else like that,' said Blizzard, a vision of Eddie Gayle in his mind. 'So how come no one collared Franz?'

'Kept moving,' said Hope. 'Arnie says the word is that Franz has people on the inside keeping him one step ahead of the game.'

'Cops?' asked Blizzard.

''Fraid so.'

'So how come you did not clock who he was at the terminal?' asked Colley.

'I simply didn't make the connection and no one had ever taken his prints so he was not on the records. Everyone assumed he was dead or living out his retirement in a villa somewhere. He's no spring chicken. I did not make the connection until I saw the newspaper cutting and by then it was too late.'

He looked at them hopefully. 'Does that sound convincing?'

'Very good,' said Blizzard reassuringly. 'It'll play really well at the official inquiry before they stick our arses out of the window to dry.'

'So,' said Colley, 'if he was yesterday's man, how come he turned up in the back of a truck at Hafton Terminal?'

'Good question,' said Hope.

'It's got to be something to do with organised crime,' said Blizzard. 'The breakout last night had all the hallmarks. They knew exactly where to go. Someone must have told them where he was.'

He looked at Hope.

'Again.'

'Yeah,' said Hope. And it won't take long for people to start saying the tip-off came from customs or one of your lot.'

'I just hope your lot are watertight,' said the chief inspector, mulling over the implications.

'Are yours?' riposted the customs man calmly.

'Point taken,' said Blizzard. 'Mind, the leak could be someone at the holding camp.'

'Whoever it was, there's a lot of top brass stamping around wanting answers,' said Hope. 'Give it 24 hours and we won't be able to move for sodding clipboards. And the Military Police are already clumping about in their size fifteens.'

'Get away,' grunted Blizzard.

'Everyone is terrified it will hit the press,' said Hope.

'I am sure they are,' said Blizzard. 'They'd have a field day. This is the kind of thing that ends ministers' careers.'

'Yeah,' said Hope. 'In fact, one of the chinless Home Office wonders rang me when I was at the camp – Sebastian Faffar-Faffaffar or something equally poncey – to say the Home Secretary had started an official investigation and that he wanted answers. Be warned, this is bringing a lot of shite down on our heads.'

'Brilliant,' groaned Blizzard. 'That's all we need.'

'So I suggest you keep your legs clean.'

Blizzard glanced at the customs man's mud-flecked trousers.

'And you,' he said with a wry grin.

'So,' said Colley, nodding at the newspaper cuttings on the desk, 'can we prove Horst Knoefler was really Martin Hasse in an earlier life?'

'There is nothing concrete,' said Hope, 'but I think there has to be a good chance. Why else would Franz have the cuttings on him?'

'Indeed,' said Blizzard, cradling his mug of now lukewarm tea. 'So, how does this sound? During World War Two, Martin joins up to escape the German plod. At some point, he realises the war is lost and he cannot go home because the plod will lift him, so he changes his name to Horst Knoefler; the police would not be looking for anyone of that name.'

'That makes sense,' said Colley. 'It explains why Hafton POW Camp had no background information on Horst Knoefler.'

'Indeed,' said Blizzard. 'And it's war so nobody cares anyway. He decides to stay in Britain, marries a British girl, puts his past behind him and turns legit. To all intents and purposes, Martin Hasse is dead and buried – as it were.'

'But brother Franz knows his new identity,' said Colley, 'and when he reads in the newspaper that Horst is dead, he comes over here to find out what happened. He can't travel the usual way in case some of Gerry's lads spot him at an airport or whatever. So he goes illegally.'

'And it looks like Garry Horton is his contact over here,' said Blizzard, his eyes gleaming. 'Which drags Eddie Gayle kicking and screaming onto centre stage. I like it, I like it a lot.'

Chapter seventeen

'I don't want to appear unhelpful,' said Edward Cranmer as he looked uncomfortably at the detectives sitting on his sofa, 'but I am not really sure I want to assist you any further.'

It was shortly after ten that morning and Blizzard and Colley had arranged to meet Elspeth Roberts and the old man at his terraced house to see if they could throw any more light on events at Hawkwith. Edward's grandson Tommy was there as well, dressed in overalls having taken time off his job as a garage mechanic. He sat on a chair in the window and looked increasingly worried at his grandfather's demeanour.

'Why not?' asked Blizzard.

'People keep getting killed,' said Cranmer. 'First, Horst, or whatever you think he was called, and now Moira Savage. I may be an old fossil, Chief Inspector, but I have no desire to go the way they did.'

His grandson nodded vigorously and Elspeth Roberts just looked unhappy, increasingly frightened by the waters in which she found herself swimming. It had been a difficult and shocking journey for a woman whose life had been spent ensconced in the relative safety of a university career.

For Blizzard, noting her discomfort, it reinforced yet again his reservations about academia. The chief inspector was well known within the force for the way he entertained grave suspicions about some of the officers with whom he worked; the ones who had been fast-tracked from university but whom he regarded as too far divorced from the realities of the street to be truly effective. John Blizzard always judged officers entirely on their ability to do the job. Although he readily acknowledged that some graduates turned into excellent officers, for which he gave them due respect, too many, in his view, floundered badly when it mattered and the chief inspector had displayed little time for their shortcomings down the years.

The way Elspeth Roberts was reacting to her situation only served to underline Blizzard's prejudices. Now, having completed his perusal of her, he looked away, a thin smile on his face, and studied Edward Cranmer.

'All we want to know,' said Blizzard, 'is if you knew Horst Knoefler was really called Martin Hasse?'

'I have told you all I know,' said the old man. 'As far as I was concerned, Horst Knoefler was who he said he was. Now, I really would like you to go.'

'But did he say anything that might suggest his real name?' insisted the chief inspector.

'Please, Mr Blizzard,' said Tommy, half getting to his feet. 'He has said all he is going to tell you. This has upset us all. He knew Moira Savage and…'

'How did he know her?' asked Blizzard.

'I was one of the people who signed her petition to save the POW camp,' said Cranmer. 'And I went to a couple of her meetings about the housing plan.'

'Why?'

'I agreed with Moira that the camp should be preserved. I wanted to help her if I could. But now...' His voice tailed off. 'Now, I am frightened.'

'And it takes a lot to scare Grandad,' said Tommy. 'Like, he went through the war and that.'

'But what scares you now, Edward?' asked Blizzard.

'This does not seem to have been a random killing, Chief Inspector,' said the veteran. 'What if this madman is looking for other people who supported Moira?'

'Did Moira ever tell you she was being threatened?' asked Colley.

'I knew there had been some unpleasant things happen to her,' said the old man cautiously, 'but that's about it. We were hardly close friends, Sergeant. We had tea at her house a couple of times, met after a meeting once, but that was about the extent of it.'

Cranmer paused and shook his head in disbelief.

'Such a terrible tragedy,' he said. 'She was such a nice woman.'

'Indeed,' said Blizzard. 'But to go back to Horst. Are you sure he never...'

'Please,' said Tommy, walking over to stand by his grandfather and fixing the detectives with a hard stare. 'We really are serious about this, Chief Inspector. People are being killed and he really does not want to be involved. He has a bad heart and the doctor has said he must avoid anything that makes it worse. Please, go.'

Blizzard eyed him for a moment but one glance at the worried expression on the old man's face and the genuine concern on that of his grandson was enough to convince him.

'I am sorry,' he said, standing up. 'I was forgetting myself. We will go.'

'Thank you,' said Edward Cranmer, extending a mottled hand. 'This really has upset me.'

'I can understand that,' said Blizzard, shaking the hand and walking into the hallway.

As Tommy opened the door, Blizzard turned back to Edward Cranmer, who was standing in the doorway to the living room, watching the detectives go with a relieved look on his face.

'Just one thing,' said the chief inspector. 'Have you ever received threats, Mr Cranmer? Is that why you are so frightened?'

'No. No, I haven't.'

'And he doesn't want to start getting them now,' said Tommy, gesturing to the open door. 'Go, please.'

The detectives and Elspeth Roberts walked along the congested little terraced street to their cars parked at the far end.

'And how are you?' asked Colley, having noted her increasingly anxious demeanour throughout the meeting.

'Terrified,' she said.

'Understandable,' said Blizzard. 'Well, hopefully our forensics boys can get something off the piece of paper with the death threat on.'

'What did you make of Edward, Mrs Roberts?' asked Colley. 'He seemed only too eager to get rid of us.'

'People are very worried, Sergeant,' said Elspeth, turning frightened eyes on the officers. 'With Moira having gone, people are thinking who will be next.'

'People?' asked Blizzard. 'Like who?'

'Everyone who has worked on the site is frightened.' She stopped walking and looked at the officers. 'Some of them knew Moira and we are widely seen as supporting her campaign to save the camp. Doctor Hamer has already ordered extra security for us.'

'Mrs Roberts,' said Colley, 'there is nothing to link your work with the murders. For a start, as far as we know, Horst Knoefler and Moira Savage did not even know each other existed.'

'I would not be so sure,' said Elspeth, reaching into her jacket pocket and producing a piece of paper.

'What is that?' asked Blizzard.

'I went through my old documents last night,' she said. 'To see if I had missed anything. I found this. They were some of the people who wrote to Moira to support her.'

'How come you have it?' asked Colley, taking it from her.

'She gave it to me a few months ago. I had forgotten that I had it.'

'Why would she give it to you?' asked the sergeant.

'She thought it might help me.'

'Help you do what?' asked the sergeant, glancing down, his eyes widening as he read the note. Wordlessly, he handed the piece of paper to the chief inspector.

'Moira knew I was researching the history of the camp,' said Elspeth. 'She said I might be able to interview the people on that list for my final report. I don't suppose for a minute it was an entirely selfless act. I imagine she hoped that if I concluded that the camp was an important historical monument, it would help her fight to block the housing development.'

Blizzard said nothing; he was staring at the piece of paper in astonishment.

'Jesus,' he breathed.

Written on top of the list in Moira Savage's scrawling hand was the name Horst Knoefler.

Chapter eighteen

'The answer is here, I know it is,' said Blizzard.

They were standing at the side of the empty grave at Green Meadow Farm. It was mid-afternoon and the winter gloom was already closing in again. After a busy day, Blizzard had felt himself drawn back to the graveside for reasons he could not fully understand. All he knew was that he felt compelled to stand by the graveside once more. He stood, staring down at the damp earth and the rain-covered blue tarpaulin stretched across the hole.

Next to him, David Colley glanced around at the foggy fields, turned up his anorak collar and shivered. He had finally to admit it, there was something about the place, and this time he could feel it, too. Could feel for the first time the sensations that had so unnerved the chief inspector that first day, the sensations that the lads who stayed guard there in the early days of the inquiry had talked about in hushed, almost embarrassed tones. Colley recalled their relief when Blizzard announced there was no further need for a round-the-clock guard there. Colley had dismissed it as fanciful talk but, standing at the grave and feeling the chill in the air, he was not so sure. Not that he was going to show it to the chief inspector. One of them had to keep their wits about them.

'What do you mean the answer's here?' asked the sergeant, trying to sound casual.

'This place is trying to tell me something, David.'

'So, what is it saying?' said Colley. 'All I can hear is that sodding wood pigeon.'

'Really?' asked Blizzard, turning to look at him intently. 'Is that all you sense here?'

'Yes.'

'Honestly?'

The chief inspector's look made Colley feel uncomfortable and finally, he admitted defeat.

'OK,' he said. 'There's something weird about this place. Happy?'

'So let's play its game,' said Blizzard, surveying the barren fields. 'Let's try to listen to what it is saying.'

'Oh, come on, guv, this isn't about bloody ghosts,' began Colley but the chief inspector silenced him with a look.

'I know it's not,' he said softly. He stared over at the fields and the distant copse rapidly vanishing into the murk. 'But have you never stood at a murder scene and felt it talk to you?'

Colley hesitated then nodded as he recalled, as if it were yesterday, long minutes standing in a murdered six-year-old girl's bedroom, her walls covered with posters of puppies and horses, the floor littered with dolls and felt-tip pens, long minutes in which he had stood in silence and fancied he almost heard her speak to him. Almost heard her voice hanging in the air, small and clear. The sergeant had thought about it many times in recent weeks since he and Jay had decided to try for a family. It was every parent's greatest fear, he had thought, and now as he stood and looked at the chief inspector, he recalled the emotions of that little girl's bedroom.

'Yeah, I have,' he said.

'It's what makes you a good detective,' said Blizzard. 'Believe it, David, this place talks to me. This is where it all started, here, in this very spot.'

'OK,' said Colley. 'Talk.'

'Thank you. Let's look at what we know. This is where Horst Knoefler died, or at least where his body was dumped, and Moira Savage was killed less than half a mile from here. They are linked by this place, David.'

'Yeah, but I really don't think we should read too much into that,' said Colley, jerking out of his reverie. 'There is no evidence that Horst Knoefler, or Hasse or whatever he's called, ever met Moira Savage. All we have is that his name is on her list.'

'Granted. But whatever happened, their deaths are connected to this place in some way, are they not? It's a circle that we have to complete.'

'Maybe there is no link,' said the sergeant. 'Maybe we are creating one where it does not exist.'

'But that would mean we are looking for two murderers.'

'I thought that was the idea, though,' said Colley. 'What did you say this morning, guv? That you fancied Henderson Ramage for Moira's murder but not for Knoefler. He was something different – that's what you said.'

'I know,' said the chief inspector. 'But that was before I came back here.'

There were a few moments of silence as the detectives stood alone with their thoughts. Colley pondered the situation. 'So where does that leave us?' asked the sergeant at length, stamping his feet as the cold started to work its way into his bones.

'I'm not sure,' said Blizzard, looking out over the fields again, as if seeking inspiration. 'But I tell you, David, this place is trying to tell me something.'

'Well, I wish it would bloody hurry up,' said Colley, flapping his arms. 'I'm freezing my knackers off out here.'

'OK,' said Blizzard. He clapped the sergeant on the shoulder and headed across the field. 'Let's go and see if we can prevail on your nice Mr Harvey to give us a cup of tea.'

'Yeah,' said Colley enthusiastically. 'And his missus does a madge fruit cake.'

'Madge?' asked Blizzard, shooting him a look as they approached the gate. 'I thought she was called Jane.'

'Yes, she is,' said Colley, looking surprised. 'I told you that half an hour ago. Is your memory going, guv?'

'No, it isn't. What the hell does madge mean?'

'It's Colley-speak,' said the sergeant. 'Short for magical.'

'Short for bloody bonkers,' grunted Blizzard.

As they were approaching the welcoming lights of the farmhouse, a figure appeared from behind the barn and started walking rapidly down the track towards them.

'That's Harvey,' said Colley, peering through the mist.

'Does he always look that worried?' asked Blizzard.

'I've never seen him this bad.'

'Can I have a word?' asked Harvey, walking up and lowering his voice conspiratorially, even though the surrounding fields were desolate and empty. 'I think there's something you should know.'

'See,' said Blizzard, turning to his sergeant with a triumphant look on his face. 'I told you this place would talk to me. All you have to do is listen.'

Chapter nineteen

'Your German was here.'

The detectives looked in amazement at the dishevelled figure of farmhand Dennis Hoare. After their meeting on the track, Robin Harvey had taken them into his cosy kitchen where they were confronted by Hoare's cowed figure. Colley recognised him as one of the workers he had seen on previous visits to Green Meadow. The sergeant remembered him because every time he approached Hoare, he looked uncomfortable. At the time, the sergeant had attributed it to the usual suspicion of police felt by many people, particularly in rural areas. You got used to reactions like that; it had taken Jay's parents the best part of two years to feel fully comfortable with him and even now, her father would say something indiscreet then clap a hand to his mouth as if he should have stayed silent. For his own peace of mind, Colley had run a check on Dennis Hoare and discovered a clean record. He had also asked around his colleagues, and officers over at Burniston, and no one recognised the name so the sergeant had dismissed him from his thoughts. How wrong could you be, he thought.

Hoare sat at the kitchen table, head bowed. He did not make an appealing sight. Aged in his mid-thirties, his lanky brown hair was uncombed and scruffy, his gaunt features grimy from a day's work and he had not shaved for several days. His skin was weather-beaten and cracked after a lifetime working outdoors. He was dressed in jeans and a green pullover and his battered cap rested on the table. But it was his eyes that made the strongest impact on the detectives. Deep pools of fear.

Hoare's appearance was in sharp contrast to his boss. Robin Harvey was a fresh-faced man in his late twenties, brown hair neatly combed, beard immaculately clipped and eyes bright but betraying concern; Robin Harvey had found himself thrust into the centre of the detectives' inquiry, and for a man who only wanted to farm and to ensure he could look after his wife and two small children, that was difficult to handle.

After making the detectives a welcome mug of tea, his wife took the children into the living room and Colley could hear, because the sturdy wooden door was not quite closed, the sound of the television. He allowed himself a small smile – Thomas the Tank Engine, if he was not mistaken. Such things were of interest to him now since he and Jay had agreed to try for a baby. Colley had not told anyone this, not even Blizzard. He was still not sure how the chief inspector would react. All these thoughts momentarily crowded into his mind as he heard the Thomas the Tank Engine music from the video which Harvey's young children were watching. Colley smiled as he heard them shout out at the screen as their favourite characters appeared.

Sitting next to him, Blizzard was not occupied with such thoughts and he eyed the crumpled figure of Dennis Hoare with keen interest.

'I take it you mean Horst Knoefler was here?' he asked.

'Yeah.' Hoare nodded.

'When?'

'Fifteen years ago.'

'How did you know it was him?'

'I overhead Mr Ramage call him that.'

'Which one?'

'Henderson.'

'I assume his father was dead by then?'

'Na.' Hoare shook his head. 'He was killed a few days later. That's how I remember when it was.'

'What happened?' asked Blizzard.

'They were walking in the field, talking like.'

'Who were?' asked the chief inspector.

'Henderson Ramage and the German.'

'How come you saw them?'

'I was there to bring a sack of summat out of one of the huts and were walking along the other side of the hedge. That's when I heard Henderson call him Knoefler.'

'Did you hear what they were talking about?' asked Colley.

'Only a bit.' As Hoare nodded his head, a lock of lank hair flopped over his eyes. 'They were talking business, like. The German fella, he said he wanted to buy some of the land.'

'Which bit?' asked Blizzard.

'The field where those prisoners are buried.'

'Are you sure?' asked Blizzard.

'Yeah. Definitely.'

'Why would he want to do that?' asked the sergeant.

'Said he didn't want to see the bodies covered in houses. Said it weren't respectful.'

'How did he know about the housing plan?'

'Henderson made no secret of it. There'd been quite a few blokes in suits looking round the place.'

'And what did Ramage say when Knoefler told him this?' asked Blizzard.

'I don't fair know but he didn't sound very pleased. Said he could get more money from housing. Then

Henderson, he sees me, and runs after me. He shouts at me, like. Trying to find out what I had heard. I said I never heard owt. He said I must never tell anyone like.'

'And you didn't?' asked Colley.

'Na.'

'Not even me,' said Robin Harvey, shaking his head at the thought of what had been happening on his farm without his knowledge.

'Why not?' asked Colley, looking hard at Hoare.

'Henderson said he would kill me if I did.' The fear was back in the farmhand's eyes. 'You don't argue with him.'

'No, indeed,' said Blizzard. 'So, what happened next?'

'I got out of there, went back to the barn, tried to forget it ever happened.'

'And,' asked Blizzard, an edge to his voice, 'did you see Horst Knoefler leave the farm, Mr Hoare?'

The farmhand hesitated.

'Mr Hoare,' said Blizzard sharply. 'Answer the question.'

'Na,' said the farmhand at last. 'Na, I didn't.'

'Thank you,' said Blizzard softly.

'There's one more thing,' said Hoare suddenly.

'More?' asked Blizzard.

'Yeah,' said the farmhand. 'There were rows.'

'Between whom?' asked Blizzard.

'Old man Ramage and Henderson. Terrible rows, they were. One time, when they were standing in the barn arguing, Henderson hits him, busted his lip. Sent him flying, it did.' He shook his head. 'Nasty business it was, seeing father and son at each other like that.'

'What were the rows about?' asked Colley.

'His father didn't want to sell the land,' said Hoare, speaking rapidly, 'but Henderson said they could get a lot of money. The old man, he said no, said the farm had been in his family for a long time and it were going to stay there. Said the Ramages were farmers and that was that. When he found out that Henderson had been inviting folks to look at the land behind his back, he was furious.'

'And that is when Henderson hit his father?' asked Colley.

'Yeah.' Hoare nodded, adding after a pause to collect his thoughts. 'Then, after it happened, Willy jumps up and shouts that Henderson would only sell the land over his dead body.'

'Are you sure that's what he said?' asked Blizzard sharply.

'Yeah. Yeah, that's what he said. More shouted it, like. He was livid. I'd not seen the old fella that angry before.'

'Then what did he do?'

'Stormed off without saying owt. When Henderson saw me, he said he'd kill me if I spoke about it. He wasn't messing, neither. Then his father gets shot...' The farmhand allowed himself a strange kind of smile, his teeth yellowed and crooked. 'You work it out, Mr Blizzard.'

'Jesus,' said Blizzard. 'You know what you're saying, Dennis?'

'Don't I just,' said the farmhand bitterly. 'I ain't slept proper for years worrying about it. Then when that Knoefler fellow were found, well...'

'But,' pointed out Colley, 'the inquest decided Willy Ramage's death was misadventure, that he fell onto his gun, probably after the dog bumped into him.'

'Pha!' exclaimed Hoare. 'Your detective inspector, Wheatley or whatever they called him, he believed anything anyone told him. He was on a different planet.'

'What do you mean?' asked Blizzard.

'Them townies knew nowt. That dog had been walking out on the lands with Willy for years, do you really think a pheasant or owt like that would spook him? Everyone knows it weren't no dog that shot old Willy.' Hoare gave a dark chuckle, his leer exposing his crooked teeth again. 'I mean, can you really see that happening?'

'No,' said Blizzard, eying him morosely, 'I don't suppose I can.'

Chapter twenty

'You want to do what?' asked Ronald, sitting forward on his chair and gaping at the detectives in astonishment.

'You heard me, Arthur,' said Blizzard. 'I want to re-open the investigation into the death of Willy Ramage.'

It was six o'clock that night and after a hurried discussion in the car on the way back from Green Meadow Farm, Blizzard and Colley had been united in their proposed course of action and were now sitting in the chief superintendent's office at Abbey Road, trying to convince him to agree. Outside, in the darkness of another Hafton winter's night, the wind was getting up and the officers could hear the rain driving ever harder against the window in the silence that had descended on the room. The detectives were not surprised that Ronald's reaction had been less than enthusiastic; such a course of action was fraught with potential difficulties.

'But why?' asked Ronald plaintively after a few seconds of pondering the bombshell.

'The RSPCA has been on, sir,' said Colley, his face deadpan. 'They think the dog was unfairly convicted. A case of wuff justice, as it were.'

Ronald stared at him for a second then at Blizzard's equally impassive face.

'This is some sort of stupid joke, yes?' asked the superintendent.

'It is a stupid joke,' said Blizzard, winking at the sergeant. 'But actually we do want to reinvestigate the death.'

'But I thought that was all done and dusted years ago. The coroner brought in a misadventure verdict.'

'He did,' said Blizzard. 'But we think he was wrong. That is why we want the case re-opened.'

'You'd need good cause, John.'

'We have good cause. We believe there is a link between the deaths of Horst Knoefler, Moira Savage and Willy Ramage.'

'You'd need new evidence.'

'We've got new evidence. A farmhand has come forward to say that father and son argued bitterly. Henderson wanted to flog the land off for as much as he could, his dad wanted to keep it all for farming. Henderson even attacked him over it.'

'And Willy told his son he would have to kill him to get permission,' noted Colley. 'A few days later, he was as dead as the proverbial.'

'And I'd have to clear it with Burniston,' said Ronald, as if he had not heard the detectives' words. 'And the coroner.'

'Then clear it with them,' said Blizzard. 'But tell them we want to do the inquiry from here because it fits in with the Knoefler inquiry. I don't want anyone at Burniston doing it.'

'And the chief constable will need telling,' added Ronald unhappily.

'Then tell him.'

'Look, is this really necessary, John?' Ronald looked at him with dark eyes. 'I mean, really? You're not just doing this for devilment?'

'Arthur, I know why you don't want this to happen and I know it puts you in a difficult position.'

'Too right it does,' said Ronald gloomily. 'Danny Wheatley is destined for great things. The word is he will be promoted to chief inspector and brought onto the chief constable's team when he comes out of traffic next month. There's even talk that he will be after my job before long.'

'God forbid,' murmured Blizzard.

'So, the chief will not exactly be delighted when he hears you want to re-open one of his blue-eyed boy's biggest cases.'

'I know all that, but if we think Danny Wheatley got it wrong over Willy Ramage, then it's our duty to check it out, whoever gets hurt, surely? Unless I am mistaken, that's our job. Isn't it?'

Ronald, who was torn so often between the need for diplomatic relations and self-preservation and the need to do the right thing, thought for a moment then came down instinctively on the side on which he always came down. Blizzard knew he would, Colley knew he would, Ronald knew he would, but they played the game anyway.

'OK,' said the superintendent. 'But, be warned, John, there'll be a lot of shit coming down on your head over this.'

'And yours,' said Blizzard.

'Don't I know it. I can't see the Burniston commander welcoming this for starters. You know what Michael Raine is like; you're hardly top of his Christmas card list after that dust-up you had with him last year.'

'I know but you've made the right decision,' said Blizzard. 'That's what makes you different from those other muppets.'

'Thanks,' said Ronald, genuinely appreciating the comment but still uncomfortable at the thought of the difficult days to come. 'I imagine you want to do the inquiry yourself?'

'No.' Blizzard gave a wry smile. 'Somehow I think that would make things worse. Besides, Tulley has turned up some new lines worth chasing on the Knoefler case.'

'Then who will you get to do it?'

'I was thinking of Chris Ramsey.'

'Why?' asked Ronald, although the tone of his voice suggested he approved.

'He's a DI, a solid officer, people respect him and he doesn't carry the baggage I do. Besides, doesn't he know Danny Wheatley?' Blizzard glanced at Colley. 'I thought you said they started out as rookies together over at Halcrombe Street? Maybe Danny will open up to Chris a bit more.'

'OK,' said Ronald. 'But listen, John, watch Chris Ramsey's back all the time. I don't want him cut adrift over this one.'

'I watch all their backs,' said Blizzard. 'You know that, Arthur.'

'Yes, I know, but you have to realise there's a lot of important people in headquarters that like Danny Wheatley.'

'It's a DBN thing,' said Blizzard.

'DBN?' asked Ronald.

'Department of Brown Nosing, sir,' explained Colley.

'Maybe so,' said Ronald. 'But whatever you think of him, Danny Wheatley is well and truly on the way up.'

'He must be,' said Blizzard. 'They've started calling him Daniel on the memos.'

'For God's sake, will you take this seriously, John!' exclaimed Ronald. 'This is as delicate as it gets. There's a lot at stake for all of us.'

'And the last thing I want to do is get anyone in trouble, certainly not you. Or Danny, for that matter. He's a good officer and no one wants him to have got it right over Willy Ramage more than me but if the force has made a mistake, we have to sort it out. You know that, Arthur.'

'Yes, I know,' said Ronald, 'I know.'

'And if the chief gives you a hard time over it, remind him that the "pledge to the public thing" he published last month banged on about accountability.'

'Somehow I might not mention that,' said Ronald, fixing the officers with a stern look.

Chapter twenty-one

Night had fallen over the city again as John Blizzard made his way wearily across the wasteland the next evening, illuminating his way with a torch and peering into the shadows, broken glass crunching beneath his feet. Behind him, beyond the ramshackle tall brick wall abutting the municipal car-park, the orange city centre lights twinkled and he could hear the low hum of traffic and the occasional blast of a car horn. Over to his left, and behind him now, the large glass windows of the railway station were brightly illuminated and the platforms inside were bustling with early evening commuters. But here on the wasteland, Blizzard felt cut off from all that, like he was in a different world. It was a sensation that he enjoyed and for many years, the engine shed had proved a refuge when he needed time to think as fire and fury broke above his head. Which was why he had come now.

It had been a testing day because, as Ronald had predicted, the news that Blizzard wanted to re-open the Willy Ramage case had caused major problems in headquarters.

It was an intervention from a surprising source that eventually swung the argument Ronald's way when the

Chief Constable seemed likely to refuse the request. Relatively new to the post of Deputy, having been appointed from one of the Yorkshire forces, Ken Bright was a no-nonsense hardened career detective, a burly dark-haired man in his late forties, a veteran of numerous murder inquiries, a man who talked straight, expected police officers to lock villains up and who had worked his way up through the ranks the hard way. Bright now proved his worth again, arguing forcefully that there was no alternative to re-opening the Willy Ramage case.

The city hall clock having just struck seven, Blizzard was walking towards the railway shed to spend some time with the Old Lady and gather his thoughts. Many a crime had been solved in the hours he spent struggling with recalcitrant bolts or standing back to look at the engine and lose himself in dreams of the day when she would steam again. Fumbling about in his anorak pocket for the keys, Blizzard was startled by the scraping of a shoe and whirled round as a figure emerged from the side of the engine shed.

'Who's there?' he called out, trying to conceal the alarm in his voice.

'The Fat Controller,' said a voice. 'Arthur said I might find you here.'

Recovering from the surprise, Blizzard peered into the darkness.

'Ken?' he said as the deputy chief constable stepped out of the shadows and into the chief inspector's torch beam. 'What are you doing here?'

'I needed to see you,' said Bright.

'You'd better come in then,' said Blizzard, unlocking the shed.

A few minutes later, they were sitting on battered old stools in the chilly shed, cradling steaming mugs of tea and surveying the old locomotive.

'She's a beauty,' said Bright. 'Or at least she will be when you've finished.'

'How come so appreciative?'

'My grandfather drove engines round the colliery near my home when I was kid. Sometimes he let me go on the footplate. Don't suppose he was allowed to but no one ever seemed to mind. I loved it. Happy days,' he said wistfully.

'Yeah,' said Blizzard, recalling his own childhood fascination with steam. 'You know, you are the first copper I have ever heard say anything nice about steam engines. Colley says I'm crackers.'

'He might have a point,' said Bright.

'Go on.' said Blizzard, 'I know you are not here to talk steam engines, spit it out.'

'OK, for a start, we never had this meeting.'

'OK.'

'And, frankly, I should not be here.'

'But you are.'

'Yes.' Bright took a sip of tea before looking earnestly at the chief inspector. 'Listen, John, there is some heavy shit coming down and I am afraid it may be about to drop on your head.'

'Meaning?' said Blizzard.

'This Willy Ramage business. There are people in headquarters want to see you out of the door over it.'

'Tell me something I don't know,' grunted Blizzard. 'It's been like that for years.'

'Yes, but this time it's different.'

'Because of Danny Wheatley?' asked Blizzard. 'Why, for God's sake?'

'He has been earmarked for great things. The chief sees an attack on Danny as an attack on him.'

'Maybe he does, but if Danny got it wrong, then surely we have to look at it again?' exclaimed Blizzard. 'That's what I said to Arthur and I imagine that is what he said to the chief. And you agree with that; I heard what you did today and I'm grateful for the support.'

'Yes, I do agree,' said Bright. 'But I'm not sure the chief sees it that way. Look at it from his point of view; he's about to promote Danny Wheatley to his personal staff, the press release is already written, and if it turns out he made a gaffe over the Ramage death, the chief will have to change his mind. You can imagine what that will say about the chief's judgement.'

'Yes, but…'

'And, he is already under pressure over Brian Savage.'

'Oh, come on!' exclaimed Blizzard. 'Surely, you're not saying that because they're in the Freemasons together, the chief wants this case dropped?'

'No.' Bright shook his head. 'No, he's too good a copper for that. Don't look like that, John, the chief may have many faults but he's not as bad as some people paint him. You might be surprised to hear that he backed you over this. He actually thinks you are a decent detective.'

'Really?'

'Yes, but when you let Savage out, the first thing he did was ring the chief and protest his innocence. And he wasn't the first, the chief has had a few calls from Lodge members since Savage's arrest, saying that they are angry at the way he has been dealt with.'

'For God's sake,' protested Blizzard. 'He set up his wife for a beating.'

'I know, and the chief told him that,' said Bright. 'All I'm saying is go careful. You have bruised plenty of egos in your time and there are some senior officers who would like nothing better than to see you drummed out of the force. This could give them just the weapon they need.'

'And you?' asked Blizzard shrewdly. 'Do you want to see me drummed out of the force?'

'You know the answer to that, John. If I had my way you'd be bloody chief constable by now.' Bright chuckled. 'When I had retired, of course.'

'Thanks for that.'

'Besides, there's something else,' said Bright.

'Top-up?' Blizzard nodded to the kettle.

'Aye, thanks.'

They stopped talking for a few moments as the chief inspector filled up their mugs with water and rooted round in a rusty old cupboard for a new box of teabags.

'So, what's the something else?' asked Blizzard once they were settled again. 'This business with Franz Hasse, I imagine?'

'Yeah. The Home Office is turning the heat up. There's hell on and all the publicity about them letting one of Europe's most wanted villains slip through our fingers has caused a lot of embarrassment in Whitehall.'

'I believe The Sun's headline was Brea-Kraut,' said Blizzard with the ghost of a smile.

'It was,' said Bright, allowing himself a smile as well. 'But this is heavy duty stuff. The Opposition is kicking up a big fuss over it and there's even talk that the Home Secretary might have to resign over it unless he can come up with some good answers pretty soon. And he may have to go even if he can't.'

'Why?'

'Apparently, there's a document floating around which shows that he was warned months ago that the detention centre was not secure. If the press get hold of that, he's dead in the water.'

'But how does this affect me, Ken? I accept we didn't clock him when he was caught but neither did anyone else and he wasn't in our custody when he escaped.'

'No, but the inquiry is looking for a scapegoat, John. Someone tipped off the gang where to find Franz Hasse and someone tipped off the press. If the inquiry finds that the leak came from within Western CID, you can imagine what that will mean.'

'Yes, I can,' said Blizzard.

'And did it?' asked Bright.

'Did it what?'

'Did it come from inside your CID?'

'I would not have thought so.' Blizzard looked sharply at Bright, alerted by something in his voice. 'Have you heard something?'

'No.'

'Then are you saying the inquiry might decide that the leak came from us anyway?'

'I'm not sure,' said Bright, downing the last of his tea. 'But if someone decides a scapegoat is needed, you or Gerry Hope are sitting ducks. I happen to know that Gerry Hope is held in high regard by his boss; can you say the same for the chief constable? He may think you're a decent detective but you're hardly his favourite person.'

'Well, it is a long time since we played golf together,' said Blizzard.

'Exactly.'

'Would the chief really stitch me up like that?'

'Who knows?' Bright shrugged. 'Depends how high the stakes are. All I'm doing is laying it out for you.'

'God, I hate politics,' said the chief inspector.

'Yeah, so do I, but sometimes you have to play the game.'

'So, what do I do now?' asked Blizzard.

'Well, as I see it, you've got two choices,' said Bright standing up and heading for the door.

'Go on.'

'Number one,' said the deputy, glancing back at him with a thin smile, 'is roll your trouser leg up, stick a hankie on your head and start learning the funny dance.'

'No thanks.'

'Thought not,' said Bright, grimacing as the door groaned when he wrenched it open. 'Then your only alternative is to bring this business to an end as quickly as you can. Thanks for the tea.'

And he walked out into the night. Behind him, John Blizzard sat in the engine shed and stared blankly at the locomotive. Suddenly, he felt very alone.

Chapter twenty-two

John Blizzard was not one to admit defeat easily, and early the next morning the POW camp spoke to him in tones that were strong and clear. Its language was the language of hate and it resonated down the ages. Blizzard heard it after a disturbed night punctuated by nightmares about dead soldiers and gaping graves; the chief inspector had finally jerked awake at 4am, sweating profusely, heart pounding, hands clammy. Finding himself unable to get back to sleep, and with his racing mind guaranteeing that rest was impossible, he took a hurried shower and drove to Abbey Road Police Station.

For the next three hours, he sat in his office, reviewing all the evidence and the reports from his team, while sipping endless mugs of tea. Unusually for him, he put sugar in them, sensing that he would need all his energies for the day ahead. The more he thought and the more he looked down at the files scattered around his desk, the more he kept coming back to one document in particular.

Blizzard reached for the report of the interview and started reading.

'Jesus Christ,' breathed the chief inspector, letting the file drop onto the desk once more. 'Perhaps *they* did do that kind of thing.'

Just then, the custody sergeant walked into the office, clutching a brown envelope. Blizzard smiled at him; they went back many years.

'Sorry, John,' said the sergeant, looking surprised and glancing up at the clock that read 6.35am. 'Didn't know you were in. How long have you been here?'

'You don't want to know.'

'What brought you in?'

'Couldn't sleep.'

'I keep telling you, hot milk and whisky, mate. But go easy on the milk, don't want to overdo things.'

'Thanks. What kind of a night have you had?'

'So-so,' said the sergeant, slumping in a chair wearily. 'Couple of drunks brought in for fighting about eleven-ish, then another three after a brawl at the Red Dragon, oh, and traffic lifted a drink-driver just after midnight...'

'Nice to see they do some good.'

'Yeah, well you're not exactly the most popular person with traffic right now after what you're doing to Danny Wheatley.'

'But I thought half of traffic don't like him?' asked Blizzard in surprise. 'Why the hell would they care if I make him look stupid?'

'Think it through,' said the sergeant. 'If you wreck his chances of promotion, they'll be stuck with him.'

'Bloody marvellous,' said Blizzard. 'Damned if I do, damned if I don't.'

Blizzard nodded at the envelope.

'What's that?' he asked.

'Bernie asked me to bring it along. Some lady brought it into the front office late last night. Bernie was a bit busy with a knob-head who had lost his wallet at the time and asked me to deliver it. In all the chaos last night, I forgot it. That's why I did not bring it in earlier. Sorry.'

'No need to apologise to me,' said Blizzard. 'You know that.'

The chief inspector was about to open the envelope when his phone rang. He listened grimly to the message from the control room operator for a few moments then stood up and reached for his jacket.

'Sorry,' he said. 'Duty calls.'

'Doesn't it always,' said the custody sergeant and ambled off to make a cup of tea.

* * *

Half an hour later, Blizzard was striding up the track to Green Meadow Farm, where he could see, through the blackness of the morning, the flashing lights of the police patrol cars in front of the farmhouse. Colley detached himself from the small knot of people standing in the farmyard and, a tall figure silhouetted by the lights, he walked briskly towards the chief inspector.

'Where was he found?' asked Blizzard.

'In there,' said Colley, gesturing to the barn, turning and falling into step with the chief inspector.

'What happened?' asked Blizzard as they made their way across the muddy farmyard.

'Robin Harvey found him,' said Colley. 'He always takes a short cut through the barn on his way to the milking shed.'

They walked into the gloom of the barn and the sergeant flashed his torch across to the baled hay at the end of the building.

'That's where he was lying,' he said.

Dennis Hoare had been found with a severe head injury, his blood staining the straw on the floor maroon. The paramedics had applied immediate first aid and he had been rushed off to the city hospital, hovering between life and death. As the officers stood and surveyed the scene, Hoare was undergoing emergency surgery.

'Did Harvey see anyone?' asked Blizzard.

'No, no-one. But I reckon he's holding something back, guv.'

'Harvey? I thought you said he was clean,' said the chief inspector.

'I reckon he is, but I'm pretty sure he knows more than he is letting on. He's just got that look about him. Like he's frightened.'

'We need to turn the screw on him, then. Any idea when Hoare was attacked?'

'The paramedics reckon a couple of hours ago.'

'Any idea why he was in the barn?'

'No to that as well. According to Harvey, he was not due to begin work until ten today. He'd worked a couple of late nights so Harvey gave him a lie-in.'

'So, what brought him here?' asked Blizzard, turning and walking out of the barn.

'No idea,' said Colley. 'Nothing makes any sense any more, guv.'

'I wouldn't be so sure about that,' said Blizzard.

It was then that the chief inspector remembered the envelope in his pocket and fished it out.

'Here,' he said as he ripped it open, 'shine a light on this, will you?'

'What is it?' asked Colley, flashing the torch.

'Left by some woman last night.' Blizzard glanced down, noticing the name scrawled on the top of the note. 'Ah, it's from Elspeth Roberts.'

'What does she want?'

'Once we knew Horst Knoefler was a fake name, I asked her to find out if she could find anything about Martin Hasse's war record, and…' Blizzard's voice tailed off as he read.

'What is it?' asked Colley, aware that the chief inspector had gone pale. 'What's the problem, guv?'

'This time,' said Blizzard softly. 'It is over.'

Colley grabbed the note from him and started reading. After going through it twice, he looked at the chief inspector with a perplexed expression on his face. But Blizzard was not there; he had been transported to a wild place, the man's place, and heard again the roar and clatter, felt the panic as the man fought for his life, heard the death rattle of his final breath. Saw the pain in his face – many faces this time, many struggles for life. The pain that comes with fear. The fear of men who knew they could never go home, would never see their loved ones again, would never feel the warmth of the evening summer sun on their back or feel the trusting embrace of a child. And in that moment, as the first glimmer of the morning light streaked the horizon above the copse, John Blizzard remembered them all. And finally understood.

'Clarissa?' asked the sergeant, glancing up from the piece of paper in puzzlement. 'Who the hell is Clarissa?'

'Clarissa,' said Blizzard, 'is a she.'

'I still don't get it,' said the bemused sergeant, looking down at the piece of paper again. 'And surely there is no way that...'

'No time for explanations now. Listen, get Tulley or someone to wrap things up here, will you?'

'Why, where are we going?' asked Colley, following him along the track.

'I'll explain when we get back to the factory,' said Blizzard as he reached into his coat pocket for his car keys. 'Come on, Sergeant, time to lay some ghosts to rest.'

Chapter twenty-three

It was shortly after 9.30 that morning when Edward Cranmer opened his front door and looked at Blizzard and Colley standing in the street.

'I have been expecting you,' he said calmly, surveying their grim expressions.

'I know,' replied Blizzard.

Cranmer glanced at the two stern-faced uniformed officers who were standing at a discreet distance a little further down the street.

'Did you really need to come mob-handed?' he asked.

'You never know in these situations,' said Blizzard as he and Colley walked into the hallway and through into the living room.

'How did you find out?' asked Cranmer. He gestured to the sofa, courteous as ever. 'Please, do sit, gentlemen.'

'Thank you,' said Blizzard. 'It was Clarissa.'

'Ah,' said the old man, lowering himself into one of the armchairs and looking at Blizzard with a knowing smile. 'Then, surely, you must know that your grandfather was on board the Clarissa the night she was torpedoed?'

'Yes, I do,' said Blizzard.

'Then you, of all people, must understand, Chief Inspector.'

'Not sure I do,' said Blizzard. 'At least, not everything. Not yet.'

'Do you know what he did?'

'Just what I read in books.'

'The reality was much worse.' Cranmer's eyes were moist. 'You cannot imagine.'

'No, but was it worth killing for?' asked the chief inspector.

'A promise is a promise. I resisted it for years but in the end, it wins out.'

'You don't believe that,' said Blizzard, eying him intently. 'Not really. Besides, times change. It all happ…'

'No.' The old man shook his head vigorously. 'No, I owed it to them. To all of them. It doesn't matter when it happened. Surely you of all people understand that, Chief Inspector?'

'Maybe,' said Blizzard.

'I promised,' repeated the man, voice breaking.

'Are you going somewhere, Mr Cranmer?' asked Colley, noticing a couple of suitcases hidden behind the sofa.

'Yes,' said the man, regaining his composure.

'Where are you going?'

'Anywhere. Somewhere you cannot find us.' Cranmer's face assumed a sad expression as he tapped his chest. 'I am not long for this world, Sergeant. We are going somewhere where the sun can shine on my last days.'

'You're not going anywhere,' said Blizzard.

'No.' He shook his head sadly. 'No, I imagine not. I wonder, do you mind if I ask how you made the link between me and Clarissa?'

'Elspeth Roberts worked it out. Stumbled across the passenger list in the local history library.'

'She was the one who told me about Frank as well,' said Cranmer. 'I told her she would not be able to keep her mouth shut.'

'When was this?' asked Blizzard sharply.

'This morning. She came round, tried to get me to give myself up to you. Said you might go easy on me if I co-operated.'

'So where is she now?' asked Blizzard.

'She's with him.' The man eyed him coolly.

'Jesus Christ!' exclaimed the chief inspector, jumping to his feet. 'Why?'

'She was a loose end.'

'What do you mean?' snapped Blizzard, already half way to the door.

'She knows too much,' said Cranmer. 'Like I told you before, it's never over. Not really.'

'Where are they?' demanded Blizzard.

'Up at the farm. After all...' Cranmer smiled at them. 'There's a grave ready dug, isn't there?'

Chapter twenty-four

The two detectives sped through the city streets in the chief inspector's car, Blizzard weaving in and out of traffic, flashing his headlights and honking his horn to ensure that vehicles moved out of the way. Before long, they were out in the countryside, Blizzard hurling the car round sharp corners, the squeal of the tyres cutting through the morning silence. Neither man spoke much on the journey but both realised that any delay in arriving at Green Meadow Farm could condemn Elspeth Roberts to death, and as they drove Blizzard rapped out orders over the radio and they listened to the constant, urgent chatter over the airwaves as other police officers converged on the scene. During the journey, Colley tried on his mobile phone to contact Robin Harvey, giving up in the end in exasperation when there was no answer from the farmhouse.

It was starting to rain under leaden skies as the detectives' car edged its way up the track to the farm and slowed to a halt next to the gate leading into the fields. The detectives got out and stood for a moment to survey the farmhouse a hundred metres ahead of them. All seemed peaceful.

'What do you think?' asked Colley, sensing his heart pounding.

'Could be in the house.'

'No, the grave,' said Blizzard, gesturing to the path leading across the fields.

The detectives set off at a run. As they brushed through damp grass along the field margins, they could hear the wail of sirens in the distance as police officers headed for Green Meadow for the second time that morning. Blizzard and Colley ran in silence for several minutes through the sodden fields. For all Blizzard's new-found fitness, Colley still easily outstripped him and it was the sergeant who first spotted the motionless figure. Glancing to his right over the hedge into the field, Colley saw him, dressed in a military jacket and standing still and silent as he stared into the grave. Colley could see that the tarpaulin had been pulled back.

Hearing the sergeant's warning shout, the man looked up and gave a startled cry. As Colley flipped himself over the gate and jumped down into the field, the man started to run across the damp earth of the field, heading towards the copse. Noticing that he was holding a wooden club down by his side, Colley slowed to a walk as he moved to intercept his quarry. As he saw Colley approaching, the man wielded the club above his head.

'Keep back!' he shouted. 'I'll do you!'

'Come on, Tommy,' said Colley, coming to a halt and eying Edward Cranmer's grandson cautiously. 'What good would that do?'

'Too late for that, I've gone too far,' said Tommy. He nodded at the figure of John Blizzard, who had appeared at the gate and was pausing for a moment or two to catch his breath. 'Your chief inspector knows that.'

Hearing the click of the gate as Blizzard entered the field, the sergeant turned and was about to shout something to the chief inspector when Tommy Cranmer struck. Moving with remarkable agility for a big man, he ran forward and swung the bat at the sergeant. Caught off-guard, Colley instinctively threw up an arm and tried to duck out of the way but the bat caught him a glancing blow on the elbow and he screamed out in pain. Staggering backwards, he sunk to his knees, groaning as he clutched his right arm. Cranmer advanced a couple of paces and stood over him for a moment then glanced at the approaching Blizzard.

'Keep back!' he snarled. 'I'll do him, I will, you know.'

'Leave him be!' shouted the chief inspector.

'Sorry,' said the man, looking down at Colley and raising his bat. 'Like I said, I have gone too far.'

Colley looked up at him in horror, which was when John Blizzard found new reserves of strength, gave a holler and ran the last few metres between them before hurling himself into Cranmer. The big man lurched backwards and stumbled, dropping the bat, and Blizzard was on him in a second. For a few moments, they struggled on the ground then Cranmer lashed out a fist and caught the chief inspector a ferocious blow to the side of the head. Blizzard let go of his quarry and rolled over, temporarily unsure where he was, and Cranmer grabbed for his bat. Colley staggered to his feet only to be caught by another swingeing blow from the club, this time across the side of the head, sending him crashing to the ground again, his mind a galaxy of stars.

'Bastard!' he hissed through gritted teeth as Cranmer started to run across the field.

'You OK?' asked Blizzard, rubbing his ear and shaking his head to clear his thoughts.

'Yeah,' said Colley, his face twisted with pain and blood dribbling from a gash on his cheek, 'never been better.'

He reached out a hand to the chief inspector and the two men hauled themselves shakily to their feet. Breaking into a run after Cranmer, the detectives noticed that over to their left, sprinting along the hedge, were several uniformed officers followed by Fee Ellis, who was catching them up rapidly. Behind her was the toiling, more rotund, figure of Dave Tulley.

'Check the grave!' shouted Blizzard, pointing.

One of the uniform officers raised a hand and veered off in the other direction. Ahead of the two detectives, Cranmer halted and stood and surveyed his pursuers for a moment before plunging into the copse, disappearing in the gloom beneath the interlocking branches of the trees. Running unsteadily, Blizzard and Colley were the first to follow him into the woodland, stopping and looking about wildly for a moment as they tried desperately to spot him. Then the sergeant gave a cry as a movement caught his eye.

'There!' he shouted as Tommy Cranmer appeared on the far side of the copse.

It was then, on the edge of the next field, that the big man caught his foot in a creeper, stumbled and fell.

'Come on!' shouted Blizzard.

They crashed through the undergrowth, ignoring the grasping barbs of branches and bushes as they closed in on their man. Now only a few metres ahead of them and having scrabbled to his feet, Tommy Cranmer turned and wielded his club again.

'That's enough,' he rasped, 'or I promise, I'll kill the both of you.'

Blizzard, still catching his breath, and Colley, acutely aware of the stabbing pain in his head and the dull ache of his arm, eyed him for a moment, pondering their next move.

'Let me deal with it,' said the chief inspector, stepping forward.

Behind them, there was the noise of Fee Ellis and other officers entering the woodland, and further in the distance, the sound of more police sirens drifting across the morning air.

'Come on, Tommy,' said Blizzard, 'there's nowhere to run.'

Tommy glanced past the chief inspector and saw that the perspiring Tulley had also reached the copse. Over to his left, he was vaguely aware of other shapes running across the field to cut him off. Blizzard held up a hand and all the pursuers ground to a halt, waiting for the chief inspector to make the next move. Cranmer eyed Blizzard, eyes a mixture of fear and fury. In the distance, the chief inspector could hear the sound of a tractor.

'I ain't going to let you take me,' said Tommy.

'We are going to have to,' said the chief inspector, holding out a hand. 'Give me the club. It's over.'

'War ain't never over,' said Cranmer, mud-streaked face twisted with anguish, fighting to keep back the tears, but grasping ever tighter to the weapon until his knuckles glowed right. 'And I ain't going to prison. I'll end it here if I have to.'

'It's already ended,' said Blizzard softly.

'It ain't,' rasped Cranmer.

He turned and ran out of the copse, out across the bare field, having spotted a gap between the closing uniforms who had run round the far side of the copse.

'Shit,' gasped Blizzard.

'I'll get him,' said Colley and set off in pursuit.

From the edge of the field, over to their right, there appeared a red tractor, driven by Robin Harvey. Spotting the fleeing figure of Tommy Cranmer, he changed direction and drove towards the running man, accelerating all the time, engine roaring. Cranmer turned and gave an alarmed shout and, as the tractor neared at speed, he stumbled and fell. It was enough for David Colley and he hurled himself onto Cranmer and tried to wrench the club from his hand. Cranmer swung a punch but Colley, releasing the pent-up anger from the blows he had received a few minutes earlier, struck out, his fist catching Cranmer clean on the jaw. Cranmer fell backwards but leapt to his feet and advanced on the sergeant, which was when Blizzard reached the scene. Robin Harvey had jumped out of his tractor and run to Colley's defence. Cranmer looked as if he were about to launch yet another attack when Blizzard intervened.

'If you keep running,' said the chief inspector, harsh edge in his voice, 'it will leave your grandfather to take the rap for this alone. Is that you want, Tommy, for him to die in a prison cell after all he has done for his country?'

Cranmer stopped and eyed him uncertainly for a moment.

'A cheap shot, Chief Inspector,' he said at length, defeat in his voice, 'but no, that is not what I want.'

'There you are. Besides…' Blizzard looked at him shrewdly. 'Men from the Hafton Regiment don't run out on their comrades. You stand side by side in the face of the enemy, don't you? Wasn't that the regiment's motto – *Stand As One*? Isn't that what this is really all about, Tommy?'

Cranmer looked at him in silence for a moment then hung his head.

'Yeah,' he said in a voice so quiet they struggled hear.

'Give me the club,' said Blizzard, taking a step forward and holding out his hand again.

Cranmer let the weapon drop from his grasp and Colley darted forward to pick it up and produced a set of handcuffs from his pocket, nimbly clipping them around Cranmer's wrists. The big man did not resist; the fight had gone out of him.

'Did you really think you would get away with it?' asked Blizzard, walking up to him.

'A promise is a promise, Mr Blizzard,' said Cranmer, sounding calmer now as he stared at the chief inspector.

'Yes, but it wasn't your promise, was it?' said Blizzard.

'It was my grandfather's promise,' said Cranmer. 'And that made it my promise. He said he did it for Harry Crooks.'

'Tell me about him,' said Blizzard. 'Tell me about Harry Crooks.'

'Private Harry Crooks, Hafton Regiment.' Tommy sounded proud to say the words, before his expression clouded over. 'Died when his troop ship went down.'

'The Clarissa,' said Blizzard.

'Yeah,' said Tommy with a crooked smile. 'My grandfather sailed on the Clarissa with your grandfather. And he died with him.'

'I know,' said Blizzard. 'I know, Tommy lad.'

'So you see,' said Cranmer, 'it *was* my promise.'

'There are other ways.'

'No.' There was hatred spitting through Cranmer's voice this time. 'No, this was the only way. And you needn't look like that, Mr Blizzard. I did it for Frank just as much as the others. I did it for you.'

'That I doubt,' said Blizzard firmly.

One of the uniformed officers emerged from the copse and walked towards them with heavy step.

'Did you find Elspeth Roberts?' asked Blizzard, noting the constable's grim expression.

'Yeah, she's battered and bruised but she'll be OK.'

Blizzard nodded and turned to Cranmer, noticing the look of savage pleasure on his face.

'No, Tommy,' he said wearily. 'You didn't do it for Frank and you didn't do it for me. Take him away, Sergeant.'

'Yeah,' said Colley, as the chief inspector started to walk across the field. 'Hey, where are you going?'

Blizzard made no reply. Staring out over the misty fields, he was transported to a wild place, the man's place, and heard again the roar and clatter, felt the panic as the man fought for his life, heard the death rattle of his final breath. Saw the pain in his face – many faces. Blizzard glanced skywards and noticed that the pale winter sun had vanished behind the clouds. At the going down of the sun and in the morning, he thought, we will remember them.

And in that moment, John Blizzard remembered them. Remembered them all.

And mourned.

Chapter twenty-five

As the SS Clarissa sailed through the clear Atlantic waters on a night in September 1942, the moonlight creating a golden causeway to mark her way, her passengers were blissfully unaware that they were taking part in her last hours. Most of them were asleep, the only exceptions the bored crew members standing watch. None of them knew that by the first streaking light of dawn, their bodies would be floating still and noiselessly in the tide.

Such a fate did not await Private Edward Cranmer, of the Hafton Regiment, the only man who would survive the sinking of the Clarissa. Perhaps his fate was worse than those who died that night, because for every day of his remaining life, he would relive those terrible events and hear the screams, his nights tortured by grotesque nightmares of the friends he left behind in the cold waters of the Atlantic. At least they only experienced it once. In his dreams, he would reach out as if he could touch them, but they were long gone and each time he awoke, it was with a sharp stabbing pain in his chest. His doctor blamed angina, Edward Cranmer knew it was guilt.

* * *

Sitting in the interview room at Abbey Road Police Station as dusk fell on another winter's evening outside, Edward Cranmer stared into the middle distance and recounted in quiet words the scenes that his mind had re-run every night, heard again the explosions and the rending of metal, the screams and the frantic thrashing in the water, the sizzle of the bullets strafing the surface of the water. Then the silence, broken only by the gentle lapping of the ocean as the bodies floated still and lifeless around him, their grey eyes appearing to mock the only man left alive in the dead sea. Shoulders bowed, eyes sunken, lips hardly moving, Edward Cranmer told his story in a voice that was hardly audible to the two detectives sitting opposite him.

John Blizzard and David Colley listened without speaking. For Blizzard, this was as much the story of his grandfather's last hours, and for the first time he was able to hear it from someone who was there. And as he listened, Blizzard was transported to a wild place, Frank's place. Colley, also deeply moved by what he was hearing, said nothing but listened in silence to Cranmer's testimony, occasionally glancing at the chief inspector with concern.

The SS Clarissa was a 17,300-ton ocean liner, constructed for a passenger line and launched amid much fanfare in 1913. Within a year, though, optimism had turned to something darker. Pressed into action as a troop ship during the Great War, Clarissa plied her trade between the English east coast and France, taking excited and optimistic soldiers to the trenches and bringing them back, wounded of body and broken of mind. Several times, she came close to being sunk but each time the U-Boat torpedoes fizzed harmlessly wide and, somehow, Clarissa survived unscathed. Some said she was charmed. Other, more experienced, mariners, said nothing. Perhaps they sensed her time was yet to come. Perhaps they knew that the sea always claims its own.

When peace returned to Europe, Clarissa went back to her life as an ocean liner, hosting parties in her dining room, witnessing cheery deck games, defying mighty storms and huge seas to ensure that her passengers reached their destinations in safety and comfort. And even though other liners sank to the bottom of the sea from time to time, Clarissa sailed on. She was, some said, a lucky ship. The mariners still kept quiet.

Then came 1939 and the advance of Hitler's Nazi war machine across Europe. Clarissa was once more pressed into service as a troop ship and in August 1942, she was berthed at her home port of Hafton for several days at the end of which 485 men of the Hafton Regiment trooped aboard ready for the journey to the desert battlefields of the conflict with Rommel and his Africa Korps. Slipping noiselessly out of the port on the evening tide, Clarissa sailed down the English Channel and joined a convoy that headed past France, Spain and Portugal, bound for North Africa, evading all the time the U-Boats which criss-crossed the sea in search of prey. Veering slightly more west than her captain would have wished to avoid a ferocious Atlantic storm, Clarissa found herself separated from the convoy and in The Azores when her time came.

Her nemesis was a proud-eyed young U-Boat captain called Martin Schwere. Unbeknown to Clarissa's crew, she had been tracked for six hours by his vessel which had slipped noiselessly through the dark waters unseen and unheard, its captain eagerly watching Clarissa's every move like a hawk as he ensured he kept well out of detection range. Martin Schwere was a ramrod-straight blond young man with Arian features and piercing blue eyes that hid a dark secret. In another life, he was a criminal called Martin Hasse and war came as a golden opportunity for him to evade increasing police attention so he changed his name and joined the U-Boat service. It was not just about escaping the police, though. Martin was a patriot, a

German who believed in Hitler's dream and who was prepared to lay down his life for the fatherland.

The young Schwere, a keen sailor before the war, soon distinguished himself as an able mariner and rapidly worked his way up the ranks, eventually being given his first command of a U-Boat. His commanders' faith in his abilities were well placed and that night, as he tracked Clarissa across the Atlantic, Schwere should have been a satisfied man. His submarine had already claimed several British vessels, three troop ships and a couple of frigates, sending them to the bottom of the sea with unerring aim. Many hundreds of men had died, many more were rescued more dead than alive from the cold waters by Allied ships. Schwere had watched the carnage with satisfaction, knowing that he was serving the Führer.

Each kill added to his growing reputation but also to his growing trepidation. Martin Schwere was a worried man. Word had reached him that his exploits had not gone unnoticed by the high command and that a medal ceremony was planned the next time the U-Boat docked, his picture due to be widely circulated as part of the Nazi propaganda effort. That was bad news for Schwere, whose dreams of an anonymous war were under serious threat and who feared that the police would arrest him next time he docked.

But all this was for the future and, as he eyed the ship through his periscope, he knew that the time had come to move in for the kill. On board the Clarissa, the troops and the crew were unaware how close the U-Boat was. Among them was newly-married Private Frank Robinson ready to join the North Africa campaign, he was allowed leave to return to his native Lincolnshire to see his new bride.

Now, Frank was on board Clarissa in his bunk, also asleep, dreaming of summer fields and village cricket matches. His was not to be as peaceful slumber, though, because shortly before midnight, Schwere gave the order to move in and the hunter-killer slipped smoothly towards the vessel, releasing two torpedoes when she was within range. The first one smashed into the bow, the second struck amidships and Clarissa lurched, throwing the sleeping men from their beds and causing widespread panic throughout the decks. Although crippled, Clarissa was still afloat, listing badly to one side, and her captain desperately rapped out orders from the bridge in an attempt to get her moving away from the U-Boat, which had now surfaced. Clarissa's gunners trained their fire on the German vessel but without effect and twenty minutes later, Schwere lost patience. Alarmed at reports that a British warship was in the area and had been alerted to the incident, he ordered two further torpedoes to be fired. Fizzing across the still sea, they found their target with deadly accuracy. Not for nothing had Martin Schwere and his crew won the respect of the fleet.

One of the torpedoes slammed into the side of the ship and with a mighty roar, a great wall of flame lit up the night sky. Clarissa, scarred and ruined, lurched even further to one side and started to tip over, and her captain ordered his men to abandon ship. He did so with a heavy heart; it was the second vessel he had lost to U-Boats on this treacherous run to North Africa. On the first occasion, he had drifted for fifteen hours before being picked up. Not so this time. Within minutes, he would be dead. All but one of them would be dead.

Martin Schwere watched with grim satisfaction as the panic-stricken crew and troops rushed for the lifeboats being lowered down the side of their ship. Those unable to scramble aboard hurled themselves into water soon foaming with their frantic thrashing, and the air was filled with the terrible cries of drowning men, many already horribly burned from the explosion. Further blasts rent the night air and the ship groaned and cried out in her pain; with a final sigh, Clarissa sank beneath the boiling waters, sucking many men down to their deaths with her. It was then that the U-Boat moved in. The survivors watched in horror as, the moonlight glinting off her sides, she moved noiselessly, majestically, grotesquely, towards the bobbing lifeboats. Standing atop the conning tower, Martin Schwere looked down on the sailors' plight, allowed himself the thinnest of smiles – and gave the order.

Cranmer paused.

'What order?' asked Colley.

Cranmer shook his head. Words were beyond him.

'The order,' said Blizzard quietly and looking at the broken man old man sitting before him, hunched over the table, 'to open up with the guns.'

'Jesus,' breathed Colley, looking at the chief inspector in horror.

There was silence as Cranmer fought back the sobs now racking his body. After a few moments, he looked up at with haunted eyes. Ghost eyes. The eyes of a dead man walking.

'Was Frank one of them, Edward?' asked Blizzard softly. 'Was he one of the men who were machine-gunned?'

'I really don't know,' said Cranmer. 'I could not see anything except…'

His voice tailed off.

'Except the U-Boat,' said Blizzard, finishing the sentence.

Cranmer nodded. 'And its captain standing in the conning tower and staring at us.'

'So, what happened to you?' asked Colley. 'How come you survived?'

'There were three of us,' said Cranmer, finding fresh strength. 'Clinging to a piece of wood, not sure what it was, bit of a lifeboat I think.'

'Who was with you?' asked the sergeant, who had now taken over the questioning as Blizzard sat in silence and composed his thoughts.

'Ronnie Illingworth and Harry Crooks. Harry was my best friend. I'd known him since we were knee high. We saw the U-Boat heading towards us. I see it every time I close my eyes. We knew they were our last moments. Schwere had already started firing on the boats. It was only a matter of time before it was our turn. That was when we made the promise.'

'And what exactly was the promise?' asked Blizzard, coming to his senses.

'It was Harry's idea. He said we had to promise that if any of us got out of there alive, we had to find the U-Boat captain and kill him.'

'And you agreed?'

'Yes.' Cranmer shrugged. 'I thought I was about to die. What difference could it make? I never meant to follow it through, didn't even think we'd survive but Harry was insistent.'

Then what happened?' asked Blizzard.

'The U-Boat approached…' Cranmer's eyes assumed a far-off expression as he relived those moments again. 'As it got nearer, we could see Schwere standing on the conning tower. I looked straight into his face and he looked back. But there was nothing, no emotion in his eyes. I swear to this day that he smiled. Then the guns opened up.'

Cranmer started to cry.

'Ronnie went first,' he sobbed, seeing again the foaming waters. 'Gave a cry and disappeared beneath the water. Then Harry.'

'But not you,' said Colley.

'I wish they had,' said Cranmer bitterly.

He paused again to compose his thoughts.

'I was hit twice,' he said, so quietly they struggled to make out the words. 'In the back and shoulder.'

Another pause.

'I went under.' Now the words were coming fast. 'It's true, you know, your life does flash before you. Then I was on the surface again and the U-Boat was heading away. All around me were bodies, floating on the surface, but there was no sign of the two lads.'

'When were you picked up?' asked Blizzard.

'Five hours later.' Cranmer's eyes assumed a glassy expression. 'Five hours in a dead sea, Chief Inspector. Do you know what that is like?'

'No,' said Blizzard with a shake of the head. 'I have tried to imagine it many times but I can't.'

'You never can,' said Cranmer. 'Not unless you were there.'

'And Martin Schwere?' asked Blizzard. 'When did you see him again?'

'About three years later, when he was brought into Hafton POW Camp with a new name. I could not believe it. I recognised him straight away,' recalled Cranmer. 'First time I saw him, playing chess with one of the other prisoners.'

'Did he recognise you?'

'No.' Cranmer shook his head. 'Why should he? I was just another victim.'

'And what about the promise?' asked Colley. 'Did you try to kill him?'

'Thought about it.' Cranmer gave them a soft smile. 'Felt I owed it to the boys but it wasn't something I ever meant to do. What would it achieve? When I left the camp, I thought that was that. I tried to put him out of my mind.'

'But you couldn't?' said Colley.

'He was always there,' said Cranmer. 'Then fifteen years ago, I saw him in Hafton High Street, coming out of a bank. Recognised him straight away. Couldn't believe it.'

'How come you recognised him after all those years?' asked Colley.

'The eyes, Sergeant. Sometimes, they looked straight through you – like you weren't there. They did it that night in The Azores, they did it when he played chess and they did it on that day in Hafton High Street.'

'So, what did you do?' asked Colley.

'I told Tommy. He already knew the story because I'd told him years before. I never thought for one moment that Tommy would react the way he did.'

'Did Tommy know about the promise?' asked the chief inspector.

'I shouldn't have told him but yes, I did. Stupid really. He had changed during his time in the Army. He saw a couple of friends killed in The Falklands and never recovered. He was very young at the time. After that, he always seemed so angry. It got worse as the years went on. That's what did for his marriage – he hit his wife. After the third time, she took herself and the kids off and he never saw them again. And he lost a couple of jobs after fall-outs with his bosses. Punched one of them. I suddenly had this idea that it would help him make his peace with himself if he could meet Martin. See that he was a man who was simply doing his job.'

'But you were wrong,' said the chief inspector.

'I didn't think I was, at first. Tommy said he would like to meet him.'

'So how did you find Schwere?' asked Colley.

'It was easy. I guessed he was over on business so I rang around a few hotels and tracked him down. Wasn't difficult.' Cranmer allowed himself a dry chuckle. 'They didn't have many Knoeflers booked in that day.'

Despite the situation, the detectives allowed themselves a smile.

'The rest was easy,' said Cranmer. 'I told Martin I wanted to see him again, for old time's sake. Didn't let on that I knew he was the U-Boat captain, of course.'

'Then what happened?' asked Colley.

'We brought him back to my house in the evening, gave him a couple of whiskies and Tommy offered to drive him to the hotel. Martin was already in the car when Tommy came back into the house and said he owed it to the men who died when the ship sunk. I was shocked, he'd been as nice as pie all night. I tried to talk him out of it, honestly I did, but he just would not listen.'

'You could have called the police,' said Blizzard.

'Tommy's my grandson, Chief Inspector.' Cranmer gave him a crooked smile. 'Besides, I'd made a promise, hadn't I? And if the truth be told, I didn't try to talk him out of it very hard; part of me wanted the bastard to die. For Harry. Does that make me an evil man, Chief Inspector?'

Blizzard made no reply.

'So, what happened then?' asked Colley.

'Tommy told me they went out towards Hawkwith. Said he stopped in a country lane and hit him with the car-jack. Buried him on the farm with the other prisoners. He reckoned that even if the bodies were dug up, no one would check too carefully if there was an extra body. Everyone knew that was where the influenza victims were.'

'They nearly didn't check,' murmured Blizzard, recalling the scepticism he had encountered when first arguing that something was not right at the grave. 'And I assume Moira Savage had to die because she knew what you had done?'

'She didn't know anything, why should she?' said Cranmer, surprised at the suggestion. 'We hardly went around advertising it. No, her death was nothing to do with us.'

The detectives exchanged glances. 'Henderson' mouthed Colley.

'There is one thing that still puzzles me,' said Blizzard. 'You say you only bumped into Martin Schwere again by accident yet our information suggests he was spooked by something years earlier, sold his house, stopped contact with his embassy, that sort of thing.'

'I may be able to shed some light on his behaviour. You see, when he spent the evening round here, Martin said that since the death of his wife, he had decided to go home to Germany. It was time to face up to his past. He wanted to see his homeland again.'

'Did he mention trying to buy the field where the grave is?' asked Colley.

'No.' The old man looked surprised. 'Why would he want to do that?'

'Said it was wrong to build houses on the grave. He wanted to stop it happening.'

'No, he never mentioned it, and even if he had, I don't think it would make any difference. Tommy's mind was made up.'

'I guess it was,' said Blizzard.

'Besides,' said Cranmer, 'Schwere never showed any respect for the men he slaughtered that night, did he?'

'No,' said Blizzard, 'no, he didn't.'

'Chief Inspector,' said Cranmer, turning fearful eyes on him. 'What will happen to Tommy?'

'Not sure. We tried to interview him a couple of hours ago but he wouldn't talk to us. The doctor reckons he may have suffered some form of mental breakdown.'

'No one wins,' said Cranmer softly.

'You're right, Edward. And for what? You'll be locked up…'

'Yes, but I will be dead in a few months,' smiled the old man sadly and tapped his chest. 'My doctor says it's only a matter of time now.'

'Maybe,' said Blizzard.

'Besides, do you really think they will lock up an old war hero? They'll send me to a home, won't they? Lots of rice pudding and dry toast and fresh bed-linen on a Thursday. Not exactly the worst place to end my days.'

'Probably not,' said Blizzard. 'But Tommy will go to jail.'

'He'll take his punishment. Something you perhaps do not appreciate. After he was discharged from the Army, he was devastated – the sense of failure stuck with him. Then suddenly, the man who killed his grandfather's best friend walks into the room. What else could Tommy have done? In Tommy's eyes, after all those years, he has proved his worth to the uniform. Remember the regimental motto *Stand As One?* Well, that's what he did.'

And, with a searching expression on his face, Edward Cranmer looked at the chief inspector as if in some way hoping to receive approval, forgiveness, understanding – something – for what had happened. Blizzard made no reply; somehow he could think of nothing to say.

Chapter twenty-six

'Hear that?' asked Gerry Hope cheerfully, reaching for the mug of tea on his desk and looking at Blizzard expectantly.

'Hear what?' asked the chief inspector, glancing around the scruffy office in bemusement.

'That sizzling sound.'

'What sizzling sound?'

'It's the sound of gonads being dragged out of the fire!' Hope burst out into laughter. 'A bit browned round the edges but OK all the same. You see, things here have been moving faster than you could ever have imagined, old son.'

'Oh, I don't know,' murmured Blizzard. 'We've not exactly been snail-mail at our end.'

It was the day after the Cranmers were arrested and the two men were sitting in Hope's office at the ferry terminal shortly after 4.30pm, the darkness gathering once more outside the window. The rain had just started to fall, squalling in off the river and flecking insistently at the grubby window. For all it was not a particularly salubrious office, Blizzard was pleased to be there; the invitation had given him the chance to escape from Abbey Road for an hour or two and the drive across the city had given him much-needed thinking time.

Since his arrest, Tommy had said nothing, his condition steadily deteriorating as he sat in his cell, rocking forwards and backwards, refusing to eat and taking no notice of anyone who spoke to him.

Despite the initial scepticism of the custody sergeant, Blizzard was convinced that Tommy Cranmer's breakdown was genuine. He had seen many a villain try to fake mental illness in his time, and felt instinctively that this was not one of those moments.

The strain proved too much for Edward Cranmer as well as, having been bailed into the custody of a local retirement home the night before, mentally and physically drained by his confession to the detectives, he collapsed in his room complaining of severe chest pains. With a severe angina attack diagnosed, he was now hovering between life and death in the intensive care unit of the general hospital.

Blizzard banished such thoughts from his mind and focused instead on Gerry Hope.

'If you smile any wider, your face will split open,' said Blizzard. 'And, pray, whose gonads are we talking about?'

'Both of ours, old son,' said Hope. 'After all, they've been sweating in the same onion bag on this one, haven't they?'

'Somehow that conjures up so many unpleasant images,' said Blizzard with a shudder.

'I'll tell you what happened,' said Hope, unable to contain himself any longer. 'Remember I said I had a mate with the police in Hamburg? Arnie, used to be a copper here.'

'Yeah.'

'Well, I got a call from him an hour or so ago. It's all hush-hush over there so I reckon your bosses won't know what I am about to tell you.' Hope grinned. 'In fact, you may like to be the one who enlightens them.'

'Enlighten them about what, though?' said Blizzard impatiently.

'Well, according to Arnie, Franz Hasse was nicked trying to smuggle himself back into Hamburg last night.'

'What!' exclaimed Blizzard excitedly, sitting forward in his chair.

'Yeah, the local cops got lucky. A traffic officer pulled over a car because a tail light was out and guess who they found hidden under blankets in the back seat?'

'This is all very good news but how does it help us? I mean, we're still suspected of leaking the info about his escape, surely?'

'Not any more, matey,' said Hope. 'According to Arnie, Hasse is tired of running and wants to come clean about everything. Arnie knew about our interest in him and persuaded Franz to talk to him before their heavy brigade arrived and whisked him away for questioning.

'For a start, he got him to confirm that his mates sprung him by bribing one of the camp security guards. Wouldn't name him but the Military Police have narrowed it down to a lad who lives near Nottingham. They are picking him up as we speak.'

'He'll not need to worry about gonads either once the MPs have done with him,' murmured Blizzard.

'Exactly, but it does mean that we're both in the clear, me-laddo.'

'Indeed it does,' said Blizzard, adding with an ironic smile, 'and I can think of so many people up at our HQ who will be so happy to hear that. Why, I imagine they'll suggest the force has a statue erected in my likeness.'

'Yeah, and I can guess where they'd like to shove it,' replied Hope.

'Indeed. Did Franz Hasse say why he was in Hafton?'

'Yeah, we were spot on, old son. He saw the stories in the German newspapers and came over to see what happened to his brother. They'd been in constant touch over the years, apparently, but that stopped fifteen years ago, of course, and he had no idea why and had never been able to find out.'

'Good stuff,' said Blizzard. 'Tell Arnie, I owe him a pint.'

'He's coming over here for a few days next month so you might have to deliver on that promise.'

'Gladly.'

'What's more...' Hope was interrupted by the ringing of the telephone on his desk.

He listened for a moment or two then replaced the receiver.

'I think you owe me a pint as well,' he said, pulling on his jacket and heading for the door. 'Oh, by the way, do you do the Lottery?'

'No, why?'

'Because,' said Hope, heading out into the corridor, followed by the chief inspector, 'our lads have just nicked Henderson Ramage. This must be your lucky day.'

'You don't know the half of it,' said Blizzard cheerfully. 'You really don't...'

Chapter twenty-seven

It was 8pm and Henderson Ramage glared balefully at Blizzard and Colley as he sat in the interview room at Abbey Road. A lack of cool thinking had been his downfall. Having lain low in Hafton since the incident at the ferry terminal, he had become spooked by a local radio broadcast about raids being planned for the division's housing estates by Blizzard's team. Everyone knew John Blizzard always came knocking eventually and Ramage finally resolved to make a bolt for freedom in Spain, where he had criminal associates. Pushing him into breaking cover was part of the Blizzard plan – the radio broadcast was a deliberate ploy – and it worked to perfection.

Having let his hair grow long and now sporting a beard and carrying a false passport, Ramage felt confident that no one would recognise him as he made his getaway, but walking through the arrivals lounge at the ferry terminal, he was spotted by a sharp-eyed customs man, who moved so rapidly that a startled Ramage had no chance to resist arrest.

He sat and glowered at the detectives. His lawyer Edward Elsden sat next to him, a glum expression on his face. Something told him that this was the end of the line for his client.

'The game's up, Henderson,' said the chief inspector.

'You can't prove nothing,' said Ramage.

'Actually, we can,' replied Blizzard. 'You see, since you disappeared, we have been doing some checking and, do you know, it all points to you for the murder of Moira Savage?'

'Na, that wasn't me,' said Ramage but the voice lacked confidence.

'Actually, it was you. You see, we went back and searched your house again last night, which is when we found your little hidey-hole in the roof.'

Ramage started.

'It's very ingenious,' said Blizzard. 'In fact, so ingenious they missed it first time around. Anyway, we got it this time and, guess what, we found your notebook as well. You know the one, the one with Moira Savage's address in it.'

'That proves nothing,' said Edward Elsden quickly. 'My client had her address, so what?'

'Indeed,' said Blizzard. 'Hey, maybe, they were in the same knitting circle, eh?'

Ramage glowered at him.

'Trouble is,' said Colley, taking up the story, 'you spelled Moira's name wrong in it, Henderson, just like whoever sent her the death threats. At first we thought it might be Eddie Gayle – he can't spell either – but our handwriting expert reckons it's definitely you. We also think you were the one who threatened Elspeth Roberts because you knew she was helping Moira.'

'Yeah, but I wasn't the one who tried to kill the Roberts woman,' said Ramage quickly. 'You can't pin that one on me.'

'So are you saying you *did* kill Moira Savage?' asked Blizzard sharply.

'No, I ain't.' Ramage looked rattled. 'I'm just saying I didn't do that Elspeth woman.'

'Stop twisting my client's words, Chief Inspector,' cautioned Elsden.

'Besides,' said Blizzard, ignoring the comment. 'We know who tried to kill Elspeth.'

'So perhaps the same person also killed Moira Savage,' suggested the lawyer.

'No,' replied Blizzard flatly. 'That was old MacDonald here.'

'You cannot prove that,' said Elsden, desperately trying to regain control of the situation. 'Even if my client had sent these threats, it does not prove that he killed Moira Savage. Surely, you arrested her husband for that?'

'We did,' said Blizzard. 'But we are convinced that Brian Savage did not mean her to be killed. No, I think that's down to your client.'

'It's all lies!' exclaimed Ramage.

'Shut it!' snarled Blizzard, fleetingly losing his temper, a rare occurrence in interviews. 'I have had just about enough of your shit! This time you are going down and if I have anything to do with it, they'll throw away the key!'

Colley looked at Blizzard in surprise and Ramage looked as if he was about to say something before a stern look from his lawyer silenced him.

'I warn you,' said Elsden, 'that unless you intend to charge my client with an offence, we are going to walk out of here.'

'Somehow I don't think so,' said Blizzard thinly, regaining his composure. 'See, I think your client thought that there was nothing more Moira Savage could do. Then she started talking about making the site a war cemetery and the housebuilder panicked, threatened to pull out...'

'Rubbish!' exclaimed Ramage. 'That's a pack of lies.'

'Well, you had better take that up with him,' said Blizzard, 'because that's what he told my sergeant here an hour ago once he knew you were in custody and couldn't hurt him.'

Ramage blanched.

'And, of course, Mr Elsden,' continued Blizzard, 'your client could not risk losing all that money. How would he pay your extortionate fees to start with?'

Elsden glowered at him.

'So,' said Blizzard, thoroughly enjoying himself, 'I think our Henderson told the housing company he would sort it then he sent the boys round to silence Moira.'

'You can't prove it!' blustered Ramage.

'Oddly enough, we can,' said Blizzard calmly. 'You see, our forensics team found a couple of fingerprints in Moira's house. Belonged to Mr Ramage's old drinking pal Garry Horton, did they not, Sergeant?'

'They did,' said Colley.

'Yeah, well pin this one on him!' shouted Ramage, leaping to his feet.

'If only we could,' said Blizzard wistfully.

'Yeah,' said Ramage, 'except, you won't find him. He's long gone, mate. And without him, I'm as free as a bird.'

'Yes, you are probably right. I imagine the plan was that you hook up with him,' said Blizzard and glanced at Colley. 'Oh, hang on, though, what were you telling me earlier, Sergeant?'

'Ooh, I'm not sure, my memory isn't what it used to be,' said Colley. 'Ah, I've remembered now, guv.'

'Then could you care to enlighten our Mr Ramage. I am sure he is dying to know.'

'Know what?' asked Ramage.

'Garry Horton was arrested by the Spanish police last night,' said Colley.

'What?' gasped Ramage.

'Yeah, got into a fight in a bar. One of their detectives rang us up when he discovered that Garry was from Hafton. Wanted to know if he was wanted. And do you know,' Colley said, 'it turned out he was. Somehow I think we'll be seeing Garry Horton back in this city after all.'

'Wouldn't that be nice?' said Blizzard.

'He won't say nowt!' exclaimed Ramage.

'Oddly enough,' said Colley, 'when the Spanish police mentioned you, his demeanour changed somewhat.'

'What do you mean?' asked Ramage.

'My client...' began Elsden.

'Your client can bloody well listen to the sergeant,' snapped Blizzard. 'Pray, proceed, David.'

'Why, thank you, guv, you are too kind,' said Colley. 'Well, as I was saying, Garry told the Spanish police that he was sick of taking the rap for you. I imagine that included the attack on those German students. You remember them, don't you, Henderson? Poor old Garry took the fall for you, didn't he?'

Ramage said nothing but stared in horror at the sergeant.

'Indeed,' continued Colley. 'Your mate Garry seemed keen for the Spanish cops to let us know he would co-operate if we mention his change of heart to the judge.'

'Oh, Jesus,' groaned Ramage, burying his head in his hands.

'I don't think my client should say anything else,' said Elsden firmly.

'No need – all he has to do is listen,' said Blizzard, a harsh edge in his voice, 'because we have only just started. You see, we also think he killed his father.'

'You have no evidence of that,' said Ramage furiously, leaping to his feet again and wagging a finger at the chief inspector. 'The old bastard died by accident.'

'Sit down!' said Blizzard.

Ramage slumped back into his chair and looked helplessly at his lawyer who was about to speak when a stern look from the chief inspector silenced him.

'Actually,' said Blizzard, 'we do have evidence that it was not an accident. See, you did not exactly keep what you did to your dad a secret, did you, Henderson?'

'I never told Garry Horton!' exclaimed Ramage. 'If he tries to say that...'

'Actually, it was Brian Savage. He has had time to think about what happened and he really is very upset about what you did to his wife. He's quite a changed man, actually. When we saw him earlier today, he told us everything. He had already said you promised to sort Moira out but this time, he told Sergeant Tulley that you admitted to him that you killed your father because he was standing in the way of the land sale.'

'Jesus,' said Ramage feebly.

'And we know you were the one who had Dennis Hoare done over at the farm as well.'

'I never did!' exclaimed Ramage but the protestations were becoming less convincing.

'Oh, we think you did, Henderson,' said Colley, the constant switching between officers helping to confuse and rattle Ramage. 'You see, Robin Harvey told us how you threatened to harm his children unless he told you what Dennis Hoare had been saying to us.'

'Anyway,' said Blizzard, 'before you had Dennis done over, he told us some very interesting things about your rows with your dad. I am sure you will be pleased to know that Dennis is recovering well and is prepared to give evidence in court.'

Ramage said nothing; his pale features said it all.

'I think I need time to talk to my client,' said Elsden feebly.

'I am sure you do,' said Blizzard. 'Oh, while I remember, there is some good news for him.'

'Good news?' asked the solicitor suspiciously.

'Yes, the person who started this all off – our Herr Knoefler – turns out to be the one person your client did not kill.' Blizzard beamed at him.

'Have you finished?' asked Elsden icily.

'Yes. Oh, come to think of it no,' said the chief inspector. 'Actually, I was thinking that in this new heart-warming atmosphere of *entente cordiale*, your client would like to do his bit and drop Eddie Gayle's fat arse in it.'

'Some things,' said Edward Elsden as Ramage looked at Blizzard anxiously, 'are just too dangerous, Chief Inspector.'

'I imagine they are,' said Blizzard. He stood up with the scraping of chair legs and walked out into the corridor, followed by Colley.

'Bloody hell, we got the bastard,' said the sergeant, punching the air as the interview room door closed behind them.

Blizzard leaned against the wall and closed his eyes.

'You look shattered,' said Colley.

'Yeah, I am. In fact…' His mobile phone rang. 'Now what?'

Fishing it out of his trouser pocket, he listened for a moment. Colley watched his impassive face but could glean nothing about the conversation and Blizzard said little apart from a muttered 'sorry, but you know how it goes' at one point.

'Who was that?' asked Colley.

'Danny Wheatley.'

'What did he want?'

'Wanted me to know that his move to the chief constable's office has been put on hold. Apparently, the chief decided it would be bad PR to promote him. Instead, he's being moved to Multhorpe.'

'I hope he can talk sheep then,' said Colley, 'because the only thing that ever happens up there is the farmers' market.'

'Indeed,' said Blizzard with the flicker of a smile.

'So how was Danny?' asked the sergeant.

'Not entirely happy.'

'That's another enemy for your list, guv.' The sergeant winked at him.

'And what difference will one more make exactly?'

'Aye, maybe you're right,' said Colley. 'Hey, I've just had a brillo idea, guv. Matty Roberts has just taken over that pub on the corner of Linklater Street. So, what do you think?'

'I think,' said Blizzard, 'that sometimes you have some excellent ideas, Sergeant. Put the word round, will you? Let's get the team down there, and I'll give Gerry Hope a ring, I owe him a pint or three. He can bring his gonads.'

'Guv?' asked the bemused sergeant.

'Nothing,' said Blizzard, clapping Colley on the shoulder. 'And you know, if I've got some change left, I might even buy you one as well.'

'Now you're talking,' said Colley as they turned back into the interview room.

Chapter twenty-eight

The wind whipped off the North Sea as John Blizzard stood and stared out over the vast expanse of dark water. Something had drawn him to the clifftop a few miles from Hafton that bright Saturday morning in May and as he stood there, he knew it was the only place in the world he wanted to be. Eyes seeking the distant horizon, his mind went back over the events of the past six months, events which had finally reached their conclusion late the previous afternoon.

Along with Colley, the chief inspector had been in Hafton Crown Court when Henderson Ramage was jailed for life for the murders of his father and Moira Savage. Ramage stared at the floor in shocked silence. For years, he had thought himself one of the untouchables; now everyone in the city's underworld knew that John Blizzard could touch them all. It was indeed job done.

Next to Ramage in the dock was Garry Horton, also jailed for life for the murder of Moira Savage, alongside another man; he tried to claim that her death was accidental and that he only meant to scare her, but the jury rejected the argument. Horton had been as good as his word and taken them all down with him.

Well, not quite all. He had not taken Eddie Gayle down; no, Eddie Gayle remained beyond the law. As he walked down the steps outside the court, leaving Ronald and Hope to deal with the media, the chief inspector had caught sight of Gayle, leering at him as he stood in front of his black Mercedes parked nearby.

'Next time, Eddie,' Blizzard shouted, 'next time.'

When Blizzard returned to Abbey Road, there was a note from the chief constable, congratulating him for his efforts in leading the investigation. Blizzard screwed it up and threw it in the bin.

Tommy Cranmer had appeared briefly in court a few weeks before, when the judge was told that he admitted manslaughter on the grounds of diminished responsibility. In a five-minute hearing, Tommy was sent to a mental hospital indefinitely. He would never come out, everyone knew that, and Edward Cranmer died in his sleep in hospital.

Ironically, Moira Savage got her final wish. Alarmed by the negative publicity, the housebuilder withdrew from the scheme at Green Meadow Farm.

The chief inspector stood and stared out over the choppy sea. Faces and images rushed through John Blizzard's mind but each time he came back to that one face, Frank Robinson smiling out of the black-and-white photograph. With a deep sigh, the chief inspector pulled the picture from his pocket and glanced down at it for a moment.

'Job done, Grandad,' murmured Blizzard, feeling his voice starting to crack. 'Rest in peace.'

And the tears suddenly came, sharp and stinging as the winds that whipped in off the North Sea. Then they were gone and, as the chief inspector's composure returned, so were the images banished from his mind. For a crazy moment, as he looked out from the clifftop, Blizzard felt an urge to throw the picture into the wind, to let it swoop and swirl until it fell into the sea to drift endlessly in the dark waters.

'No,' said Blizzard with a quick shake of the head, slipping the picture back into his pocket. 'No.'

He turned away from the cliff edge and started to walk back to where Fee had been standing at a respectful distance, watching him in silence.

'OK?' she asked, noticing his red eyes.

'Yeah,' he said, slipping his arm into hers. 'Yeah. Edward Cranmer was right, you know. It is over.'

'Good,' said Fee, then grinned at him. 'Hey, I realise it's the dreaded exercise but do you fancy a walk?'

'Do you know,' said Blizzard, 'I think I do, Fee.'

'Come on then,' she said, kissing him softly on the cheek, 'old timer.'

And, arm in arm, they set off along the windswept cliffs.

Character List

Hafton officers:

Detective Chief Inspector John Blizzard – head of Western Division CID
Detective Sergeant David Colley
Detective Inspector Graham Ross – head of forensics in Western Division
Detective Inspector Chris Ramsey
Detective Constable Fee Ellis
Detective Constable Dave Tulley

County force:

Deputy Chief Constable Ken Bright
Detective Superintendent Arthur Ronald – head of CID in the southern half of the force
Gerry Hope – customs officer

Other characters:

Edward Cranmer – war veteran
Tommy Cranmer – his grandson

Paul D'Arcy – lawyer
Edward Elsden – lawyer
Eddie Gayle – Hafton criminal
Franz Hasse – criminal
Robin Harvey – farmer
Dennis Hoare – farmhand
Dr Richard Hamer – archaeologist
Horst Knoefler – former German POW
Garry Horton – Hafton criminal
Henderson Ramage – Hafton criminal
Peter Reynolds – Home Office pathologist
Elspeth Roberts – archaeologist
Moira Savage – chair of Hawkwith Parish Council
Brian Savage – her husband
Malcolm Watt – council officer

If you enjoyed this book, please let others know by leaving a quick review on Amazon. Also, if you spot anything untoward in the paperback, get in touch. We strive for the best quality and appreciate reader feedback.

editor@thebookfolks.com

www.thebookfolks.com

Also by John Dean

In this series:

**STRANGE LITTLE GIRL
THE RAILWAY MAN
THE SECRETS MAN**

The DCI Jack Harris series:

**DEAD HILL
THE VIXEN'S SCREAM
TO DIE ALONE**

Made in the USA
Lexington, KY
05 September 2018